She

The Constant
Correspondent

A Sherlock Holmes
Resurgent Mystery

J. B. Varney

DEDICATION

To Debbie Rife and to Lana, my loving wife.

The Constant Encouragers!

"The game is... still afoot!"

This book is printed in Baskerville Old Face Font.

The Sherlock Holmes Resurgent Mystery Series

Book 5

"The game is... still afoot."

J. B. Varney is the 26th Great-Grandson of Alain Chartier and Thiphaine, daughter of Eudes le Maire, Chamberlain to King Phillip I of France. This same Eudes went on Pilgrimage to Jerusalem on behalf of the King and received the famous "Privileges of St. Mard" as a result, for him and his line. Mr. Varney is descended through the first five Chartier Lords of Boissy Le Sec, Essonne, Île-de-France.

He is also the 25th Great-Grandson of Thomas Arderne and Ellen de Bohun, herself the great-great granddaughter of Henry I, King of England, who was the son of William I, "The Conqueror".

Contents

Chapter 1 – The Science

In all the years for which I have case notes recorded there has been one which I have never considered placing before the public. Even despite Holmes' strong opinion to the contrary I've held my ground for years.

As a rule my friend rarely interjected his wishes or opinions into my process, other than to criticize one of my published stories. One might be too florid and another too focused upon the sensational at the expense of the logical, but always I could count upon disapproval.

The strange case of the Constant Correspondent was, however, an exception. In the beginning he often inquired generally about which case I was planning upon publishing next. In time a slight nudge began to be felt but only by way of a question regarding the case.

"What of the Constant Correspondent?" He'd ask, several years on, "have you any idea of it in the near future?" Or some such thing.

I always replied with my opinion that the case in question was far too sensational, gruesome, and grotesque and that, for a man whose own irritation at my stories had focused most upon the former aspect, that of sensationalism, I found it strange that he continued to ask after this one case.

His retort was initially silence but in time he defended it for its singular features and for the many instructive illustrations it presented regarding the science of deduction.

His points were not lost upon me, however, and I reviewed them in as much detail and fairness as I could. With so many other cases which achieved the positive without as much of the grisly and brutal which the case of the Constant Correspondent presented, I never felt my hand forced and it remained buried in my files.

When, after the passage of many more years my friend again mentioned the case, out of the blue as it were, I determined to press him for his true goal.

"You have so rarely taken an interest in my stories prior to publication Holmes, that I cannot fail to note the continued interest you have shown in this strange case. In particular your obvious and continued desire to see it placed before the public. What is the reason, for it seems so counter your usual criticisms."

I could tell that he didn't welcome the discussion and would have much preferred it if I would simply have conformed myself to his wishes, but there it was.

"To begin Watson, it presents us with what you must admit is among the most unusual cases of our long career."

I agreed, although I stated that this point alone hardly justified its publication when considered against the crux of most of my friend's harangues, that of my sensationalism. Which I said was something that the horrific case of the Constant Correspondent was brimmed full of.

"Then there are the innumerable instances it affords to highlight the science of deduction. You cannot deny that."

"And yet it does so through the most astonishing means which can only make my story one which, after I submit to the publishers, you will delight in condemning."

"Not so Watson, not so."

In his impassioned defense my friend had unwittingly given something away. We had now been together for nearly two decades and I was an avowed an expert upon Mr. Sherlock Holmes.

"Ah, I see," said I.

"What do you...see?" he replied, but I could tell that he knew I was close to his secret.

"Why would you want this most sensational of our cases made public, when you doubtlessly know there is no way for me to avoid that aspect in my telling of it? And why would you go so far as to practically pledge that you would not criticize or condemn it for its sensationalism, even before I've begun laying it out? You often say that the truth is uncovered in asking the correct questions and now I've asked them, have I not?"

Holmes had baffled me from the beginning and yet I was indeed close to discovering the real reason he had pushed so long for it to see the light of day.

"I can see by your smile that you are well-pleased with yourself but allow me to say that there are times when I miss that Watson of our early days. That man hung on my every word and marveled at my results without comprehending my deeper self. You have now, by toil and time, come to see too deeply. Yes, if I must say it, you have asked the correct questions and now I am forced to admit the truth of it."

"And not a moment too soon, I might add, and I can't help but wonder if it would not simply have been easier to do so from the start."

My friend simply stared at me from his chair and puffed upon his Turkish.

"Yes, quite," he said finally, refusing to give me any satisfaction in my moment of victory. "I have already shared with you the actions I took back in '88 to aid Scotland Yard with the Whitechapel Murders," said he.

"Yes, for what little good it did."

Scotland Yard had locked Holmes out of the investigations of the Whitechapel killings in '87 and '88, turning him into a virtual persona non grata and even threatening the careers of any of the inspectors who dared speak his name. I had still been naïvely trusting of our institutions at the time and viewed the entire business as nothing less than a shocking and shameful miscarriage of bureaucratic powers.

Then his words struck a chord in my mind and I knew exactly why he had increasingly pressed for the publication of the case.

"That's it isn't it?" said I confidently. "It's the Ripper Business all over isn't it?"

"It's true that the handling of this case stands in stark contrast to that of the Whitechapel Murders," he admitted.

"It even took place in Whitechapel!"

"And yet Watson, it was never publicized in the manner the Ripper was and it never caused the public firestorm and frenzy that case did."

"And in the case of the Constant Correspondent you were in charge," I declared. "You want the public to see the facts of the case so they can compare it with the handling of the Whitechapel Murders."

"There is only one reason you can use that phrase Watson, 'The Whitechapel Murders,' without confusing people."

"What?"

"The Whitechapel Murders."

"Indeed," I exclaimed, realizing how right he was, "and it all stems from your mastery and control in the case of the Constant Correspondent."

Then something else occurred to me.

"There were even multiple murders in our case, gruesome and twisted, all that sensationalism I had described, but you never allowed it to be publicized in the manner of that other business. Had Scotland Yard overseen that it would have preceded the Ripper Killings and been known as 'The First Whitechapel Murders.' That's why you've want it printed."

"There are many lessons to be learned from the failure to catch the Ripper, Watson."

"And the facts of the Constant Correspondent will do that?"

"I believe so," said he, "and if such a fiend should ever appear again I would hope that the comparison in approaches might prove valuable."

Sherlock Holmes' peculiar qualities had only really begun to be known with the publication of my early stories. Until then he had mostly been an oddity around Scotland Yard. My stories had not only made him a household name throughout the kingdom, but they had also forced Scotland Yard's leaders to finally, if reluctantly, acknowledge him. It had become increasingly difficult for them to dismiss him as an amateur or as unofficial. Now that I understood his reasons for pressing me on the case in question I felt a rare freedom to write as I chose. There were, as the reader will shortly find out, startling aspects and gruesome details as well, much as those of Jack the Ripper, which have also helped to stay my hand. While I cannot ignore those points I will focus my main thrust upon illustrating those powers of logic which Holmes utilized and the remarkable results he achieved.

I take only two liberties, both of which are intended to protect the innocent. The first is to cloak the Scotland Yard Inspector behind the name of "Caldecott" and to give false names to the other officers involved. In working with Sherlock Holmes many members of the established forces were placed in situations where the standard rules were sometimes set aside for what I will call the ultimate good. The other step I take is to leave the year unmentioned. This, alas, is only a slight shield over the case, to be sure, and the diligent seeker will soon discover all, but it will afford some added protection for the innocent.

It was a bright spring day in the years preceding the infamous case of Jack the Ripper and Holmes was involved at his workbench in some abstruse chemical test, the results of which would likely determine the life or death of a certain person in a much-attended poisoning case.

I rose from my own labors and went to inspect the mail upon the table. There were the usual lot of notices and one cheap envelope which could have been purchased at any general shop but it stood out for the graceful sweep and regularity of its script. It was addressed to Mr. Sherlock Holmes and I found myself attempting to apply my friend's methods. From the angle I judged the writer a right-handed man and due the steadiness of the hand I estimated an upper age of no more than 40 years. I looked at the back for thumb prints upon the seal but found none.

"What do you make of it Watson?" said he.

I started for he had his back to me and I examined the room with a quick glance. I'd been with him long enough now and the silver coffee-pot had etched his techniques firmly indeed. I knew he had used a framed picture, angled correctly, almost as effectively as a mirror upon more than one occasion, but nothing stood out to me.

"A personal letter for you, by all appearances."

"Would you read it out for me, as I have my hands full at the moment."

I sat down and opened the envelope making certain that nothing which might provide us a clue fell out and then unfolded the letter, which was itself upon inexpensive stock.

"Mr. Holmes," it began unsurprisingly, but that was where the letter left the ordinary behind. *"You*

don't know me and I am a man of no importance to anyone except my employer, and he couldn't function without my services. My only significance to you, Sir, lies in the fact that I mean to kill. Only a few additional clews for the great man are in order.[1] I live in Whitechapel and have done all my life. I'll likely die in this place as well and probably mere blocks from the humble ramshackle of my birth, which I pass by almost daily. I have no education at all, other than what I have given myself, but I pride myself, as you do, upon my logical mind. I will kill seven times Mr. Holmes. The only thing that will comfort you in knowing this is that all my victims are the very worst of men and selected for this one characteristic. They are all acquaintances of mine. Lastly, Mr. Holmes, a little incentive for you. Should you fail to stop me in time, there will be an eighth victim, Dr. John Watson. Be assured that I will write regularly. Your Obedient Servant, The Constant Correspondent."

Holmes was at my side within the first two sentences and took the letter when I finished. He approached the window and used the sunlight to aid in a minute examination of the letter and envelope.

"Odd that," said he at last.

"Odd," I exclaimed, "it is the work of a madman, surely."

"I don't believe so," he said after a long pause.

"What then? Can you seriously say that a sane

---

[1] "clews," archaic Victorian term for "clues," although while the former was going out and the language was becoming increasingly standardized, both were still being used.

person could write such an epistle?"

Holmes didn't answer. He went to his chair and pulled his large convex lens from its case.

I hadn't moved from the table but my heart was racing. The sentence where he declared that I'd be his eighth victim, not surprisingly, filled me with concern.

"Holmes?" I called after a few minutes.

"A true technician," he noted.

"A what?" I asked.

"A technician Watson," said he, "a man of rare discipline and to think he is wholly self-educated. A remarkable achievement really."

"I'm sorry," I said, "but you will have to forgive me as I find myself unable to admire the work of the man who has threatened my life Holmes."

"Indeed Watson, that is impossible to lose sight of. As disconcerting as it may be to you my dear fellow, this is my process."

I understood what he was saying and no one appreciated his effectiveness as I did, but I must admit I was shaken by the coolness with which Holmes had accepted the threat.

"What do you mean, about being a technician?"

Holmes came to the table and sat down opposite me, flattening the letter out in front of me and upside-down to him, so that I could read it.

"Follow me through the letter," he said, and then began to read it aloud, stopping in certain places.

"Mr. Holmes, You don't know me and I am a man of no importance to anyone except my employer," he stopped.

"Each of these words has been written out smoothly Watson, all in one action and with no pauses or hesitations. When he begins again however, note this dot upon the back of the letter stock."

I looked at the point and turned it over again and again. Then I noticed other similar dots spaced out upon the back of the paper.

"What is this, some sort of code?"

"It's too early to say, but wherever he adds a significant suffix or prefix the man pauses his pen, just for a moment, but always. You can't notice the pattern on the front of the letter, where all appears smooth and uninterrupted, but you can see the spots where the ink has bled through upon the back. Were this expensive stock no doubt these would remain invisible to us. See here Watson, at the word 'couldn't.' He pauses after the 'd' then takes up again and finishes."

Then he began reading again, pointing out each stopping point as he did so.

"and he could • n't function with • out my services. My only significance to you, Sir, lies in the fact that I mean to kill. Only a few addition • al clews for the great man are in order. I live in Whitechapel and have done all my life. I'll like • ly die in this place as well and probably mere blocks from the humble ramshackle of my birth, which I pass by almost daily. I have no education at all, other than what I have given myself, but I pride myself, as you do, upon my logical mind. I will kill seven times Mr. Holmes. The only thing that will comfort you in know•ing this is that all my victims are the very worst of men and select•ed for this one characteristic. They are all acquaintances of mine. Last•ly, Mr. Holmes, a little incentive for you. Should you fail to stop me in time, there will be an eighth victim, Dr. John Watson. Be assured that I will write regular•ly. Your Obedient Servant, The Constant Correspond•ent."

"But Holmes," I said, "what is the significance?"

"For now it is enough to note the discipline of man's mind," he replied. "There may be more to it, as you asked, is it a code, but for now it is enough to simply know that we are dealing with a most disciplined mind."

"I still say he's a madman."

"Or he may be a mad man Watson, and as sane as either of us."

"A 'mad man'?" I muttered, placing the pause between the 'mad' and the 'man,' as Holmes had done.

"Yes, mad, as in angry. Note if you will who he targets."

"Yes," I countered, "me!"

"You, alas good Doctor, are only the stick to make sure I'm suitably engaged with his plan."

I stared at Holmes for a long moment and wondered how his mind comprehended so much from what, to me, was so little and so painfully plain.

"Look here," said he, beginning at a new point in the letter. "The only thing that will comfort you in knowing this is that all my victims are the very worst of men and selected for this one characteristic. They are all acquaintances of mine."

"Do you see it Watson?"

"His victims are all bad men, excepting me of course, and I rather hoped I'd been upon the right track all these years."

"More than that," he said, ignoring my comment completely. "'They are all acquaintances of mine,' he says. This is not an impersonal act of random slaughter. Something in every one of these men has troubled our Constant Correspondent and the weight of it has recently become enough to launch him upon this path. His goal is to rid the world of seven evil men."

"Then why make me the eighth man and why engage with you at all. Why not simply commit the murders about which he boasts and remain hidden in the crowd. Why on earth challenge you, of all people, to stop him?"

"Now there you've done it my good fellow. You've gone and asked the critical question, why challenge me?"

"Exactly, that's what I'm asking?"

"But you have no idea as to the answer."

"Of course not, how could I?"

"Let me ask you an old question then, in the hope it will help you arrive at the answer. Why would Scotland Yard forbid my input upon the Ripper Murders when I played a critical role in dozens of other cases upon which I was involved?"

"We've already resolved that Holmes. You said it was because they didn't want to solve the Jack the

Ripper case."[2]

"Just so Watson. There is no other logical reason for implementing so complete a lock-out of Sherlock Holmes from the case?"

"Alright, but what has that to do with this, this Constant Correspondent and his murders?"

"If Scotland Yard kept me in out because they didn't want to solve the case, then does it not hold that this man has called me in because..."

Holmes let his words trail off. He wanted me to reason for myself and declare my thoughts aloud.

"Then this man has challenged you to stop him...in the hope that you will! Can that really be?"

"Indeed it can and I believe it is. So far from being a madman my dear fellow, it appears to me that man struggles with a conscience. Based upon his words there is no lack of cause for him to want these men dead. Yet some part of him recognizes the wrong in what he plans. He wants to be stopped and no doubt your stories of our cases presented him with the perfect mechanism to achieve that."

"So he means for you to stop him? You are that mechanism," I said, more confused than ever.

"Indeed. Either that Watson, or he means to defeat me in the challenge."

"Then, if it be the former, the clews he's providing, he means to give himself away?"

"On the contrary, unfortunately, for our man not only has a most disciplined mind but a keen intellect and if we are to run him to earth Watson, he means

---

[2] "They All Love Jack" by B. Robinson, Harpers Pub., ©2015.

for us to work for it."

"Then...that's why he made me his eighth victim, to see that you truly put the work in to stopping him."

"Of course. Consider it after all. How many law-abiding citizens would attempt to stop a man intent upon killing seven of the worst men in the world? Would they not rather congratulate him upon a job well done once he was finished?"

"No doubt and buy him a beer."

"Whoever he is, he is torn between his two selves. The one means to kill and to defeat me in the challenge and the other wants me to stop him."

"Then this man is a kind of Dr. Jekyll and Mr. Hyde?"[3]

"And clearly intelligent Watson. Either he is naturally gifted in intellect and has added to it by dint of hard work or he has arrived at a similar place purely through his efforts. The one thing is certain and that is he has not rested upon any inherited laurels, so to speak."

Within the hour he'd left in a disguise and I knew he was bound for Whitechapel.

---

[3] "Dr. Jekyll and Mr. Hyde," by Robert Louis Stevenson, ©January 1886.

Chapter 2 – The Crucifixion of Gam Tzomides[4]

In the small hours of the morning I was awakened from a deep sleep only to find Holmes, wrapped in his purple paisley dressing gown,

[4] The "tz" in Greek makes a sound closest to "J." Tzomides would be pronounced "jo-my-dees." Source: Thoughtco.com, "Pronouncing the Greek Language" by Nancy Gaifyllia, 2020.

leaning over my bed like some spectre, candle in hand.

"Come now Watson," said he, "It's Inspector Caldecott and the game is afoot."

Little did I realize then but Holmes' words were literally true, our game had used the darkness of night in Whitechapel as his stage and now he really was afoot. We ventured across town in the police carriage while the inspector gave us the details.

"It's a bad one Gentleman and I won't pretend it isn't. The victim was found at 1 AM by the patrolman on duty on Three Colts Lane in Whitechapel, a short distance east of Bethnal Green Train Station."

"Near Corfield Street?" Holmes enquired.

"The next to the east, Coventry Street, and he was strung up on a wooden fence, or gate rather, looking like the crucified Lord himself. Oh, and a message had been painted on the gate, religious."

"What did the message say?"

"Wages of Sin, Mr. Holmes."

"Book of Romans," said I.[5]

As we rattled across London, Holmes sat in silence until he'd finally made up his mind to take a certain action.

"Inspector Caldecott," said he, "you know my reputation and you must decide whether you want to be tied together with me on this case or not. I have information, and my insights of course, which I will share with you. In return you will follow my

---

[5] Romans 6:23.

directions on how you manage the crime scenes and reports to your superiors."

"Mr. Holmes, did I hear you correctly that there will be more crimes of this nature?"

"I'm afraid there will."

"And you'll only share your information with me if I agree to your terms?"

"I must insist upon that, if we are to bring this killer in."

"I couldn't possibly do that Mr. Holmes, not without trusting my men. I happen to know that they are heavily inclined toward trusting you more than they do our own superiors, but it is still a great risk."

"And as such you may make your own decision Inspector for, as you say, it is a risk and only you will pay the consequences. I may be censured and even run off for a time, but you could face the loss of your job and the ruin of your career."

"That sounds a terrible thing Mr. Holmes, but I happen to know that I've risen as high as I'm likely ever to see. May I ask what kind of information you have before I choose my sides?"

"We received a letter from the killer yesterday and in it he not only shared his plan with us and said he would continue to write."

"I say, that is...unusual is it not?"

"He seems a most unusual man," Holmes said.

"Well then, I suppose it's like marriage then," Caldecott said, shaking us each by the hand.

"How is it like a marriage?" I asked.

"For better or worse, Watson," Holmes replied.

"Indeed, for better or worse now. Have you the

letter as I'd like to get a look at this man's mind."

Holmes handed everything across and Inspector Caldecott, as workmanlike an officer as you'd find at the Yard, looked it over for several minutes.

"Well, that's something I've never seen the like of in all my years. A madman Mr. Holmes?"

"That was my exact opinion as well Inspector," I confided.

"I tend to think him sane," Holmes announced, "although obviously troubled and torn regarding the situation he finds himself in."

"I should say for he's just trussed up a human being like a turkey and for the whole world to see in a few hours."

With this Caldecott handed the letter back to Holmes.

"Now you must act as if you've never seen this?"

"I understand your rules Mr. Holmes, even if I remain in the dark on everything else. This man says he'll kill six more and perhaps throw in the good Doctor for safe measure," he said, nodding in my direction, "but you say he's sane?"

"It is not a small distinction; I assure you both. For the sane man, even if he carries out the same actions as the unbalanced mind, does so in a completely different way and for different reasons."

"If you say so Mr. Holmes, I guess. As you'll soon see, sane or not, he knows how to kill a man."

When we arrived on the scene we found a single policeman posted and a heavy tarpaulin thrown over the gate. Lifting it up the Inspector held a lantern and Holmes began his methodic search.

"His name is Gamaliel Tzomides, Mr. Holmes. A local tuff known to our officers as 'Gam.' He apparently thought of Three Colts Lane as his own little kingdom. He took a toll on anyone he could intimidate. He did quite well out of it although we were never able to make anything stick. One of my men said the locals generally made a detour of four blocks to avoid him. His cronies, of course, had free passage."

"A wife and children?" Holmes asked.

"He was apparently liberally minded in that area but was especially hard on the women he took up with and he never kept one for long."

"Let me guess," I said, "you were never able to make anything stick on that front either."

"We can't force witnesses and victims to work with us Dr. Watson. If they refuse to make a statement and testify, I dare anyone to make them do it, even you Sir."

I understood the Inspector's point and I knew that frustrations of this kind where his daily lot. It couldn't be easy to look at a woman beaten black and blue and not be able to punish the guilty culprit.

"So no idea who he's taken up with now?"

"No Mr. Holmes but we'll begin canvassing in the morning. It shouldn't take long."

"What's that behind the gate?" I asked.

"A two-hundred-pound anvil Doctor. The yard back there is the workshop of a farrier and he keeps a forge and anvil for his work.[6] The killer moved the

---

[6] Farrier, a horseshoer and often a general blacksmith as well.

anvil behind the gate using a wheelbarrow, then lifted it up onto a small table. He rigged it to the rope he slipped over Tzomides' head, then kicked it over. The weight pulled the victim right up there on the gate and may even have snapped his neck before it came to a stop. The killer has a ladder back there too. No doubt he slid under the gate and got everything he needed from the shop. Afterward he tied ropes to the victim's wrists and hoisted them into this crucifixion position you see here. Then no doubt he did the painting."

"He would've had to be a strong man to lift that anvil," I said.

"And thin and lithe to get under that gate," Holmes added. "No pocketbook, money, rings, or necklaces on the dead man?"

"Nothing Mr. Holmes, not even brass knuckles, the killer stripped him of everything. We'd started to think of this as a case of robbery as well as murder but your letter strikes that down. All I can say is, if the killer was looking for a bad man to be his first victim he sure picked a good one."

In the lantern light Holmes began his own search of the body and then the surrounding area. I always enjoyed watching his method as it was at times like this that he was most like a bloodhound.

He took off one of the shoes and found that the shoestrings were actually wires which could be used for many different purposes including picking a lock. Under the inner sole of the right shoe was a flat, metal blade filed to a razor sharpness. The left shoe held twenty pounds in various bills. Sewn loosely into one of Gam Tzomides pant cuffs was a brass key.

"I'm going to say that this key goes to something about which Mr. Tzomides' current lady friend knows nothing," Holmes said as he handed it to Inspector Caldecott. "The L & M stamp will no doubt match a security box at the London & Midland's Bank."

"I'll wager you're right on that Mr. Holmes," Caldecott agreed.

Holmes found another blade in the left sleeve cuff and several playing cards in the right cuff. The last of his discoveries were several metal plates sewn into the man's wool vest and beat into various forms that fitted to the small of the back, the abdomen, and one over the heart.

"Your results are embarrassing Mr. Holmes. Half the time I don't know how we missed them and the other half I can't imagine how you find them."

"That is a simple puzzle Inspector. I expect to find something and you and your men do not."

"So our expectations predict the outcome?"

"It is elementary Inspector and may be stated in one of the simplest of mathematical equations."[7]

"Someday Mr. Holmes, I very much want to sit down with you and find out how it is you know all that you do."

"In the meantime the body needs to be dealt with and the message on the gate needs to rubbed out. By the time passersby begin to flow through

---

[7] The term "self-fulfilling prophecy" was trademarked in 1948 by Meyer Schkolnick, aka Robert Merton.

here it should look like nothing happened here tonight."

"And my report?" the Inspector whispered.

"Death by strangulation with a hemp rope, one inch in diameter. Simple and straightforward."

"Indeed," Caldecott replied uncomfortably.

"And if you will join us in the morning at Baker Street. We can discuss our findings."

"If I still have a job tomorrow morning, I'll see you there Gentlemen."

Holmes was in one of his contemplative moods after we left the Inspector on Three Colts Lane. The diabolical and grotesque nature of what I'd just witnessed had left my mind reeling. Receiving a threatening letter had been one thing but to see it acted upon so swiftly and so fiendishly was another completely. I'd seen murder before and the terrible violence of war, but there was something about the killing of the man upon the gate which somehow went beyond all the others. The brilliance of the man's plan couldn't be denied, even when it was murder about which we were talking. Meanwhile it had been a design of such simplicity; an anvil, a rope, a small table, and a short ladder.

"You saw to the gate?" Holmes asked when Inspector Caldecott joined us in the morning.

"All according to your instructions. Although have you not considered how upsetting this will be to the killer, your Constant Correspondent? He painted that message for a reason and as to the body, could you imagine what the public reaction would have been had they seen it? In the form of the Salvatore Mundi of all things!"[8]

I had to agree. It was unbelievable what a two-hundred-pound weight could do to the human neck but to see the man, Gamaliel Tzomides, hung in the exact position of Jesus upon the cross was jarring. It would have inflamed all of London.

"You are quite correct Inspector. I have no doubt that the crucifixion of Gam Tzomides upon that gate in Three Colts Lane was our killer's masterpiece. It may even have been the fruit of years of planning and thinking. He meant for it to be seen, to make an impression. I know that, but I believe he will accept that the better player has bested his opening chess move."

"And will he not retaliate Holmes, as Inspector Caldecott has envisioned?"

"He will realize his three mistakes and will adjust his second murder accordingly, to eliminate these, but no, you and I are not in danger. He will stay true to his script which outlines the rules."

"So I am only in danger if we are unable to stop him by his seventh killing?"

"Correct Watson."

"And what are the three mistakes?" Inspector Caldecott asked, "for as I see it the murder of Gam Tzomides was the perfect crime. I mean, we have nothing on his killer."

"I have to agree Holmes. This seems to have been the masterpiece you said he wanted it to be."

"You are both looking at this murder from the

---

[8] Salvatore Mundi: Savior of the World. Inspector Caldecott was referring to the position of Jesus crucified upon the cross.

perspective of an officer and a friend of the law, of men burdened with and by the responsibility of solving crimes and delivering criminals to justice. That probably can't be helped either, considering your backgrounds and experience in the law. The killer however had goals beyond the killing, goals he very much wanted to achieve. First and foremost he wanted the killing to be seen by the public. In light of that his first mistake was to commit the crime too early in the night."

"I see, giving us time to react."

"In fact Inspector, it allowed you so much time that you were able to come here to Baker Street and enlist our aid."

"So you don't think he foresaw that?"

"Indeed not, for he imagined waking to a city in uproar, with banner headlines declaring the brutal crucifixion of a man in England of all places. Instead what does he find?" Holmes said, handing the London Illustrated News over.

"Gladstone introduces Irish Home Rule Bill," I read aloud, "the House of Commons will debate but Lord Churchill vows that Ulster will fight the passage."

"Not only is the leading news not his, but it also isn't even dealing directly with England."

"He'd be furious," the Inspector agreed.

"The second mistake was the placement of the crime to a backstreet with little traffic during those hours. This was especially true of Three Colts Lane as, thanks to the Inspector, we know that people avoided that area, going as far as four additional blocks because of Gam Tzomides' toll."

"Yes, but no doubt he had no choice in either the location or the time of the murder Holmes. As we know it was both the time and place his victim frequented, and no doubt Tzomides would have retired soon anyway, forcing the murderer to act when he did."

"Yes, he had little choice from the perspective of the opportune crime, Watson, and he gladly took the lonely location and the early hour. Both made the murder easier for him. However, doing so did thwarted his greater goal. The killing of Gam Tzomides was primarily meant to stir London into furor."

Then Holmes pointed at the paper.

"I have no doubt that Ulster will fight the Prime Minister's bill," he said glibly, "and I could probably predict its failure in the House, if you and your old friend, Colonel Hayter, are looking for the odds upon a wager. But this stuff will not do, not for our killer."

"I see, so it is a choice between committing the perfect crime or creating a disturbance across the city and the country?"

"He is just now realizing that. You can be certain he will adjust his plans to better fit his goals now."

"He could not have foreseen my bringing you in Mr. Holmes, and that has cost him."

"Indeed Inspector and that is his third mistake. He believed that I would be left out of the immediate investigation, that Gam Tzomides would be seen, that word would spread, and a furor of terror would erupt. His choices as to time and place allowed us to counter his purpose and foil him and this is the same model we must follow as long as we hunt this man. Next time we will not have the luxuries we had last night, I'm certain of it, and you must be ready to act without us Inspector."

"But why does he want to cause such disruption Holmes, for I thought his goal was to kill seven devils!"

"It is an excellent question Watson and to answer it I will ask you a question in turn. Do we all agree that our killer could simply have seen to the murder and departed without the trouble of the painted message?"

"Yes, of course," I agreed.

"And he would have fulfilled the words in his letter, the killing of seven bad men, or devils as you so floridly put it Watson."

"Yes," the Inspector replied.

"Then the answer to your question, Watson, is to be found in the message he left us upon the gate."

"The Wages of Sin?" I asked.

"That's correct. He wants to punish the seven devils just as he wrote and you pointed out. He wants to see the guilty punished once and for all. Who knows how he knew Mr. Tzomides. Perhaps he was bullied into paying the toll every day or maybe they were neighbors at some point. Could the Constant Correspondent have watched Gam Tzomides beat a woman that he, our killer, cared for? We don't know, but we do know that two of his clews were that he knew all the men he would kill and that they were all of the worst kind. By painting that script, 'Wages of Sin,' we know what message he wanted to give London. No doubt he wanted bad men to think twice, but even more, I believe he wanted to father a general uprising against crime in London."

"A champion of the people?" the Inspector said in wonder.

"Of a sort and certainly a catalyst to change, and no one can argue that crime is rampant across London, especially in the poorer areas."

"So he sees himself in the role of what the Americans would call a vigilante," I offered. "And since in his view the law has failed to punish men like Tzomides, no offense Inspector Caldecott."

"None taken Doctor."

"But since the law has failed to punish these kinds of men, he is taking the law into his own hands. Not only that but he sees himself as merely the first of a movement."

"And I expect the same or a similar message to be visible in the location of his next murder. The crucifixion of Gam Tzomides was meant to be his masterpiece and the location of the murder fit perfectly with that means of murder. Now that it was foiled he will, I believe, attempt to replicate it elsewhere."

"And this time it won't be in a remote location will it Mr. Holmes?"

"And it won't allow you time to contact us either Inspector. He is playing a chess game with me. The first win was to our side. He will not want that to happen again."

"Yes," I said, "but as I see it, while we foiled his broader plan we've done nothing to hinder his next murder or even to learn anything that could help us find our killer."

"I understand your concerns Watson," Holmes replied patiently, "but remember that his victim of last night and those yet to come, are not honorable and innocent men. The tragedy in the crime, it might be argued, doesn't exist and the world is a better place for the absence of one or all of these men. Yes, the killer's actions violate establish law, but few would argue that he has committed a 'miscarriage of justice' in punishing these men."

"So, in a sense he has actually achieved justice," Inspector Caldecott replied.

"As you said, if his work could have been seen he very well may have been seen as a champion of the people, Inspector. And contrary to what you believe Watson, I assure you that we've learned a great deal."

"Such as?"

"Our man is lithe, agile, and strong."

"But couldn't a hundred thousand other men in London fit that description?"

Holmes ignored my interruption.

"With that he is also intelligent, disciplined, and meticulous. Taken together that makes him a man of between 25 and 35 years of age, with the high odds upon his being someone between 27 and 32."

"I say, that is very helpful Mr. Holmes."

"He travels with a carrying case. This too will function as an eliminator of a great many people."

"How do you figure on the carrying case?" the Inspector asked.

"Did you find any paint or brush at the crime."

"I see. No, we didn't. So he carries some of his supplies with him. Interesting."

"We know he wears smooth-soled dress shoes so he is not a laborer or even a craftsman."

"Wait a moment Holmes, I didn't see any footprints like that?" I noted.

"But Watson, were you looking for them?"

"No," I had to admit, "I wasn't."

"And I was and I assure you there were a dozen such prints upon the ground, the ladder, and the small table he would have pushed over from the ladder after setting the noose, and even Inspector Caldecott doesn't wear such light footwear as you can see."

We all looked down at the Inspectors heavy-soled walking shoes.

"Beyond this our man wears a long, lightweight raincoat of the dark blue color which is currently referred to by the faddish name of 'Continental Blue'."

Here Holmes opened a small paper and handed over a half-inch patch of dark blue material.

"From the underside of his sleeve when he reached across the top of the old gate to set the noose and only a fraction of a second before he kicked the anvil over. That was on an old nail."

"A new coat and an old nail, this is brilliant

Holmes," I said by way of an apology for believing that we'd learned nothing from our visit to the place of the murder. Now I recalled my early suspicions and doubts regarding my friend's methods. Upon one instant I gave him a test, to deduce the history of a watch which had belonged to my father. Despite the difficulty Holmes had taken on the challenge willingly enough, but his findings were so numerous and so accurate as to reek of charlatanism. I had ended by accusing him of using the most disgraceful means of finding out about my brother, only to then present his findings at a later time as proof of his genius. I was soon set to rights and he showed that he had no previous knowledge that I even had an elder brother. The experience left me humbled and apologetic. A few years on I'd come so far as to expect wonders from him.

"All of this is quite...astonishing Mr. Holmes, and it will help us get our man."

"Dr. Watson is correct though Inspector. If not in the number he proposed, then at least in the principle he espoused, for no doubt there are many strong, fit young men who work in offices or stores as clerks and tellers, running about London on any given day in dark blue raincoats with smooth-soled dress shoes and carrying cases."

"Is there anything else you might point me to that could help us?"

"Other than the fact that our man is five feet seven inches tall, with dark brown mid-length hair and a bandaged left hand, I can think of nothing else at this time."

As I said, Holmes had so often dazzled that I'm afraid that I had come to take it all for granted, but the tour de force which we had just witnessed was truly breathtaking. Inspector Caldecott and I now stared in absolute silence.

"But how Mr. Holmes?"

"After shimmying beneath the gate our man stood with his back against the bricks of the archway before proceeding. From this imprint upon the wall I could easily estimate his height, plus-or-minus an inch. At the level of his head I found these caught in a bit of rough mortar," he said, handing over the folded paper along with his convex lens.

Upon opening the tissue paper I spied two dark-brown hairs of approximately four inches in length.

"And you discovered all this in the dark," I said in disbelief.

"I did have a lantern Watson," he replied with a smile, pleased that I had been so impressed.

"And the bandaged hand?"

"As you kept the rope you will find a profusion of blood upon the rope which held Mr. Tzomides' right wrist.[9] The only blood upon the dead man was a light tracing around the neck where the rope had tightened down. As there is no blood upon the rope used to tie the left wrist that had to be the first one

---

[9] Just a reminder: Tzomides is pronounced "jo-my-dees."

he tied up. I noted a significant crack running with the grain of the wood in the side rail of the ladder, the left side, and a discoloration of fresh blood upon that area. It holds that when he'd finished tying up the first wrist and moved the ladder to the right side of the victim he pierced his hand upon this wooden dagger. When he tied the second wrist in place, the portion of the rope which was touched by his left hand absorbed a large amount of blood."

Holmes handed over his white handkerchief at this point.

"I pressed that into the rope and came away with a substantial stain. I estimate he'll need to wear a bandage upon that hand for at least three days and likely longer."

Chapter 3 – You've Done Me For

"Mr. Holmes," the second letter began just as the first. *"You won't catch me you know? Even if you succeed in running me to earth, I shan't be taken in nor will I swing for what I've done. History will have no record of such things for me. This is a fact upon which you may rest most assuredly. I am quite resigned to my fate, should it come to that, and you will see me play the sportsman as well as any of your class at University.*

I'll be so bold as to prophecy my own death. I will die in Whitechapel, mere blocks from the place of my birth, but I shan't be kept like a base animal in some distant prison. You shan't do for me as you have for so many others. There will be no drum rolls or black flags for the Constant Correspondent, you may put that from your mind altogether.

By now you've learned about my first murder and how deserving he was. No doubt you didn't expect it to follow upon the heels of my first letter so rapidly, but I pride myself upon my competence and energy. So you must learn quickly and be prepared for the next one.

As London screams for justice what are the poor bobbies to do? There is so much smoke for so little fire. They are such bunglers. That is why I came to you Sir. In you I have a truly worthy opponent. You must accept it Mr. Holmes, we are two faces of the same coin. We both want justice, but you cannot deny that my methods will achieve that goal while you remain merely a Scotland Yard Stooge.

Only six more until I get to your friend. Your Obedient Servant, The Constant Correspondent."

"A nasty piece of work that," I commented, "but he clearly knew nothing of our activities of last night Holmes."

"No, but you see he had to get the letter posted to have it here today. He was forced to make his assumptions about the case and clearly he saw no possible issues. He makes his error painfully obvious however, does he not Watson, with that phrase, 'As London screams for justice.'"

"Indeed he does."

Inspector Caldecott had departed after our early morning meeting and Holmes and I had waited for the post, to see if anything would arrive from our correspondent. Now my friend got into his disguise, that of a bookseller which he had used before to good effect and wished me luck with my task as he closed the door behind him.

Armed with a Colton & Company map of Whitechapel I was to visit shops and businesses along Whitechapel High Street, staying alert for a young man of Holmes' description. I felt especially certain that I could identify everyone with a bandaged left hand. At the New Year I'd purchased Stevenson's "The Strange Case of Dr. Jekyll and Mr. Hyde." I had since read it twice and been struck by the author's gifts.

"Here," I thought, "was literature." Against such I felt my simple efforts pale.

Yet, as grotesque and unearthly as Stevenson's fictional Mr. Hyde was, our villains were flesh and blood. The crucifixion of Gam Tzomides had left me with the feeling that I'd opened another door into the dark soul of evil. It wasn't merely because of the genius in the method of the noose and anvil either, although that couldn't be denied. It was that I'd realized for the first time that anyone out there, in any shop, store, or business, was capable of imagining and implementing murder. That chilling notion stayed with me as I walked London's streets in search of the young man with the bandaged hand.

After several hours I'd grown quite bored with my labor and had not seen so much as a single bandaged hand save for that on a beggar old enough to be our man's grandfather. Then I spied the sign of a bookshop near the Osborn Street crossroad. It was one of those narrow fronted three- and four-story affairs with the awning out front and a large sign above.

"Chartier & Co. Books," it read and I had the pleasant thought that it might renew my interests. I could do no worse than I had for a half-hour break from the monotony.

I followed an older couple into the shop and was struck once again by my love of books, of new books and old, large and small, biographies, atlases, journals, and adventures. Even the smell of old books seemed to fill my head with ideas.

The shop owner, for such I took him, greeted the couple in French and introduced himself.

"Monsieur Sharle Chartier," said he, standing tall and with a natural nobility of bearing about him. I wandered in and was pleased to find a used copy of Stevenson's Jekyll and Hyde, in good condition and tolerably priced. I took it up. I would present it to Holmes upon his forthcoming birthday.

I then made my way to a section on Scotland and began my search for anything of interest. I often began this way in new bookstores and had moved on to the section on expeditions. A few minutes later I was joined by the regal man himself.

"Good afternoon Sir. Sharle Chartier at your service," he said, as if Sharle were a hyphenated part of his surname. "May I help you find anything?"

"You wouldn't have a book on Forsyth's First Yarkand Natural History Expedition would you?"

The topic had interested me for some time but I had never thought to pursue the purchase of the

volume before now. The presence of the nicely stocked little shop of used books had prompted me.

"T. D. Forsyth led the expedition into the area of Eastern Turkestan in 1870?"[10]

Danton-Sharle now looked around apparently unsure of himself, and then apologized.

"I'm sorry but the clerk who oversees that section is presently away at lunch," then looking at his watch he added, "He should return within the quarter hour if you would like to continue looking until then. Or I can take your information and send you a card if we have it?"

---

[10] "Lahore to Yarkand – The Yarkand Expedition of 1870 under T.D. Forsyth" FIRST EDITION – by George Henderson and Allan Hume. Published in London by L. Reeve & Co. ©1873.

I made my excuses and complimented the man upon his shop, promising to come again at a better time, then returned to my duties. I had been correct about visiting the bookstore, it had reinvigorated me and I continued very much a new man afterward.

The following morning we met again at Baker Street with Inspector Caldecott and reported our mutual failures to uncover any likely candidates for our killer.

"The papers are quiet so it looks like your correspondent took the night off. I have to say though, that second letter is an insulting piece of tripe, 'what are the poor bobbies to do? There is so much smoke for so little fire. They are such bunglers,' and he doesn't ignore you either Mr. Holmes, you are 'merely a Scotland Yard Stooge.'"

"It does seem that Dr. Watson is the only one to escape this round," Holmes laughed.

"No doubt I'll get double come tomorrow!"

"No doubt," Caldecott agreed, "but this will shock your senses Gentlemen. That key stamped with L & M, well, it did belong to a security box at the London & Midland's Bank. And can you guess what we found in it?"

"Money?" said I.

"Yes indeed Dr. Watson, money and lots of it. Five hundred and sixty-three pounds and change to be exact. Gam Tzomides was a wealthy man, no question, and here am I an honest Inspector at the Yard and I can't put a scratch on his fortune."

"No doubt you aren't the possessor of a London & Midland's strong box either Inspector," Holmes replied.

"No surprises there, but as to our plans for tonight, do you believe the killer will strike again Mr. Holmes?"

"I rather think he will," Holmes muttered. "His loss in the first round required an adjustment to his plans and methods, but he warned us that he warned us after the first letter."

"That's right," I agreed, "'no doubt you didn't expect me to follow upon the heels of my first letter so quickly,' he said, or something like that."

"I pride myself upon my competence and energy. So you must learn quickly and be prepared for the next one," Holmes added.

"It looks like he was the one who needed to learn, after his first disappointment," the Inspector pointed out.

"Tonight will be different," Holmes admitted, "you're right about that Inspector. Plan on a thoroughfare which is heavily traveled with early morning traffic, as he now knows he needs his audience. Wagons, carts, cabbies, peddlers and people walking on their way to work, that's what he wants. He'll strike with as little time as he dares give himself, leaving your men less time to communicate the killing to you and, he hopes, no time for you to erase the scene before the crowds arrive. He's counting very much upon the tedious process of communicating to the Yard, getting an Inspector out, and making a decision. If your men act quickly and independent of the usual falderal we may foil him a second time."

"In which case Mr. Holmes, by the time this lunatic gets to Murder #3 he'll roll the victim out right in front of the morning crowd, leaving us helpless to counter him."

"You are more correct than you know Inspector and that is why I've compared this to a chess game."

"Or a boxing match Holmes," I offered.

"Very true Watson."

"Is there anything else Mr. Holmes?"

"I doubt if he'll have time for the evenly spaced message he left us in Three Colt Lane, but he'll leave your men something to remove no doubt."

"We've already purchased the turpentine and I assure you we'll do our best. You might be surprised to find out that my superiors were happy with my last report, the clear case of strangulation with a hemp rope."

"I'm not," Holmes replied, "they dread anything out of the ordinary as it requires greater thought and involvement, and therefore greater responsibility. Make sure your men record the details well, in the absence of being able to examine the crime scene in detail their efforts will be doubly valuable."

"I've prepared them and if it's possible well make use of the tarpaulin again, just as we did before, and allow you to work your talents Mr. Holmes. Are you going out again today?"

"I am," Holmes said, "but Dr. Watson has duties which require his attention."

Holmes had spoken of my practice, which while still admittedly modest did have its pull upon me.

Late that night Holmes returned disappointed

and clearly weary of his labors.

"What is it?" I asked.

"Despite your notion that the city of London would be brim full of fit young men matching our description Watson, I saw only 4 men today who showed a bandaged hand. Of them two were older than I and only one, a costermonger with hobnail boots, fit our age and had one upon his left hand."[11]

"So likely not our clerk in a Continental Blue raincoat with smooth-soled dress shoes."

"No, not likely," said he, disappearing into his bedroom.

I was awakened in the grey light of early morning by pounding upon the front door and found a Police messenger and carriage awaiting me.

"Sir," said he, "Mr. Olmes wonders if you might join him and Inspector Caldecott."

"I think you are mistaken officer," I replied, "for Mr. Holmes is asleep upstairs."

"No Sir, 'ee ain't. Mr. Olmes is at Old Montague and St. Mary's Street, where there's been another killing."

I tried to place the location with my groggy mind. "East of London Hospital?"

"Aye, that's right Sir, and 'ee asks you hurry."

When I returned, dressed as best I could in such a limited time, the same man handed me a note.

As the coach lurched into action I opened it and read out its contents.

---

[11] Costermonger: a street seller peddling a wide variety of goods from a wheelbarrow, handcart, or donkey cart, usually working a fixed route through working-class neighborhoods.

"You will be dropped at the synagogue across Whitechapel Road from St. Mary's Church. Proceed to Old Montague where you will come upon a great crowd of onlookers. Inasmuch as it is possible memorize every face you see for I have no doubt that the killer will be one of those gathered there. He will want to see his work and hear the reactions of the people. If he realizes you've seen him his first reaction will be to turn and flee. Do not pursue him Watson for I assure you that he will be armed with a powerful weapon and more than willing to use it."

The coach did very much as Holmes said and in the early dawn I walked up St. Marys Street upon the backs of the staring crowd.

"What is it?" I asked one of the men there.

"Someone was kill't," said he bluntly.

"T'were Big Pat Langford," a woman wrapped in a heavy shawl said, turning toward us, "the boss o' the McAuley's. That man said 'ee seen 'im."

The McAuley's were a Whitechapel gang that specialized in running a protection racket over many of the areas businesses. You either paid or you knew you'd be "paid a visit."

That was when I saw the man in the crowd and realized that he'd seen me. He turned and vanished into the sea of faces, a dark-haired man in a top hat, in a sea of dark men in top hats, in the dim, early hours of the morning. I continued to mingle for another half-hour and not a single person reacted as that man had.

I pushed through the crowd and one policemen,

recognizing me, pulled me through. As I drew up to Holmes he asked if I'd had any luck.

"I'm afraid not," I admitted, still looking into the faces in the crowd.

"That's unfortunate, I thought we'd see him."

"So what happened here?" I asked.

"This is the Queen Street Grain Warehouse," Inspector Caldecott replied as he joined us and shook my hand. "Whitechapel Station is just up the road and every morning they unload two freight cars of grain and bring it here in wagons. From all I can gather it was near five this morning when all of this happened."

"One wagon had just emptied out," Holmes added, "and another was due in a few minutes. Some of the sacks of grain were still stacked along this wall to be moved into the warehouse. The two men on this end of the process were both in the warehouse. One of them said he heard a bang and assumed it was the rear gate of the next wagon being dropped open."

"He said it surprised him that they'd arrived so early, as their goal is to have all the sacks from one wagon transported into the warehouse before the next wagon arrives."

"But when he came out here again there was no wagon," I replied.

"That's correct Dr. Watson. There was a huge man sprawled upon the grain sacks, his back against the wall, covered in blood. He was holding his stomach."

"And the man was already dead?" I asked curiously, for in my sad experience such wounds didn't kill immediately.

"No, he lingered for a short time but the wound was...horrendous. The only words the warehouseman heard were, 'You've done me for!'"

"You've done me for!" I repeated.

"And a small revolver hung from his right hand," Holmes continued, "but it hadn't been fired."

"And was it this Langford fellow, of the gang?"

"Big Pat Langford of the McAuley Gang, a big man who had the habit of keeping his right hand tucked into his vest," the Inspector said, "like the great men in their portraits, only now we know what was kept in that vest."

"The pistol?" I asked.

"That's right Doctor."

"This time the message was hurriedly scrawled in white paint Watson," Holmes said, "Beware the Judgment!"

"So it was similar to the first one," I replied, "Wages of Sin."

"Well I hate to tell you this but some of this crowd were early enough to recognize Langford and no doubt they saw the scrawl upon the wall."

"It couldn't be helped I'm afraid, but we still hope to avoid tomorrow's banner headlines at least," the Inspector said.

In the cab on the way back to Baker Street Holmes took the time to describe the cause of death.

"So he was shot at close range," said I, "and in the abdomen?"

"Yes Watson, but the wound was...odd."

"Odd, in what way?"

"It appeared that Mr. Langford was killed by...a shotgun and it is difficult to believe that such a man, armed as we now know he was, would let anyone walk up on him with a shotgun."

"And how is that odd?" I asked, "for a shotgun, cut down, could have been easily concealed."

"Yes, but the wound showed an unusually tight pattern and a powerful blast. A shortened shotgun," he paused.

"A shortened barrel has a larger pattern," I said.

"He bled profusely Watson and the testimony of the warehouseman says he lingered only two or three minutes and was largely incoherent during that time," Holmes pointed out, knowing that my experience with wounds would be helpful.

"While we would generally expect such a wound to bleed out more slowly and for the victim to remain conscious for an extended period, I see," I replied, considering everything I heard.

"This case," Holmes muttered quietly, "it has its difficulties."

"Well, another terrible man is dead and as far as that goes our correspondent has proven consistent."

"Yes, but does it not strike you as odd that the methods used in the murders are so different?"

"Almost like two different killers, is that what you mean?

"The first fits with what I would expect from a small man who has had all the time he's wanted to design his method of murder. The second shows none of the finesse and control of the former and simply reverts to the blunt brutality of the firearm."

"Well, you did say he would have to adjust his method if he had any hope of getting his message out to the public, and to tell you the truth Holmes, I expect we'll read about this in the evening paper."

"There is that" he mumbled, but I could tell that something was troubling him.

Inspector Caldecott joined us midday, exhibiting an excitement I'd not seen in him before.

"Gentlemen," he said after being shown in, "you must come and see this and tell me how this could have happened for I am all at sea."

With that he took one of our large napkins and spread it out upon the table, giving it the general shape of a bird's nest. Then he took an envelope and poured out its contents in the center of the napkin and stepped back to allow us a good view.

"This is what was taken out of the victim at this morning's post-mortem."

"How is this possible Inspector," I asked.

"You mean, how was Big Pat Langford killed by a .42 caliber bullet and 14 custom sized buckshot pellets, when only on shot was heard by the warehousemen? Yes Dr. Watson, that does present us with certain...problems doesn't it. Still, the man holds to his testimony and declares there was only one shot."

"We begin to arrive," Holmes said, returning to his chair."

"What do you mean?" I insisted, for what I saw made no sense to me at all. "Two killers shooting simultaneously?"

"You know Watson, you possess the remarkable ability to illuminate the darkness."

"Really Mr. Holmes," Inspector Caldecott said as he took a seat upon the settee, "unless you are about to tell me that I must now go in search of a second killer, I don't see what is so remarkable in the good Doctor's speech."

"No Inspector, there is not a second killer to pursue and it is true that Dr. Watson's 'speech', as you called it, is completely incorrect. However, his words do shed a powerful light upon the solution, if you would like to try and discern it."

"Two killers shooting simultaneously might have possibly resulted in the sound of a single bang, but that would have been long odds indeed and as you say, that hypothesis isn't correct. So, since a second killer doesn't exist, what else could have achieved the same result?"

There was a long pause as he considered and then his face brightened.

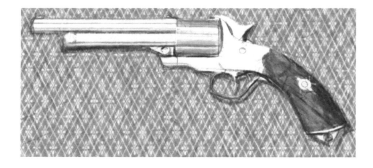

"One killer firing two weapons simultaneously, one a pistol and one a shotgun!"

"I'm afraid that would have required the longest of odds as well Inspector, but it was a good try."

"But Holmes," I declared, "if two killers and two guns was incorrect, and one killer with two guns was not the solution either, I don't see a solution."

"Think instead of a gun which is actually two guns Watson, incorporating both the revolver and the shotgun together, and firing simultaneously for the simple reason that they are detonated by the same trigger."

"But such a gun doesn't exist and would surely be impossible to build Mr. Holmes."

"Have you ever read my monograph upon handheld revolvers Inspector Caldecott?"

The poor man shifted in his seat but could not bring himself to answer Holmes.

"No, for if you had you would know that the French-made LeMat Revolver combines a nine-shot, .42 caliber revolver with a 20-guage shotgun."

"So the answer is a single killer with a single gun firing the .42 caliber bullet and the 20-guage shotgun off the same trigger, therefore simultaneously," I said in amazement.

"Right you are Watson, our killer had a LeMat."

"I've never heard of it Mr. Holmes, but you say it was made in France."

"Designed in America by a Frenchman-turned-American, produced in Belgium and France, and shipped to the Confederate States via the port of Birmingham, England, during the American Civil War. And now quite clearly in the hands of someone in Whitechapel with whom we have to deal. A bit of a puzzle that."[12]

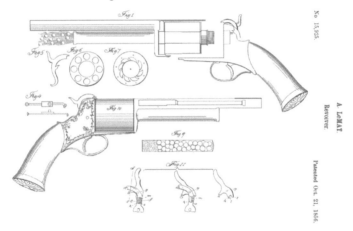

"So that's how it was done, two shots, one explosion," Inspector Caldecott muttered almost to himself.

---

[12] The LeMat revolver was designed 1856 by a Frenchman who had moved to New Orleans, Louisiana. His name was Jean Alexandre Le Mat, and his revolver was produced in Paris, France, by Frederic Girard & Son.

"And that was why the victim transpired more quickly than usual, the bullet lodged in his spine."

"But how did you know that Dr. Watson, it's true, it did, but I didn't say it."

"Simple," I said, feeling very much as I imagined Holmes must feel all the time, "a bullet of that caliber would have easily passed through the man's abdomen unless it had struck bone."

Chapter 4 – Two Devils Down

"Nothing in the early posts Watson," Holmes remarked after the Inspector's departure.[13]

"Our man must be behind his times, but you seem troubled Holmes."

---

[13] The postal service of Victorian London would pass the same locations several times a day, from approximately 7:30 in the morning onward. This allowed for multiple deliveries.

"It's this case," he muttered quietly, "two men of seven have been dispatched in quick order and outside their being 'the worst kind of men', as our correspondent called them and as you noted earlier, the only commonalities between them is that they were both murdered in Whitechapel and both were left with a message of warning."

"But you expected adjustments, in fact, you predicted that he'd have to change his method."

"Indeed," he murmured, "but I expected the killer's signature to come through, like that of a master artist."

"You mean, like the noose and the anvil?"

"Precisely, like the noose and the anvil. There was such obvious consideration and geometry to the method. The knowledge of the victim's habits combined with the overwhelming force and speed provided by the method used. Even the posing of the body in the form of the crucified Savior, it all spoke of a high degree of mastery, of finesse even."

"And the killing of Langford, shot point blank range and left right where he fell against the wall, bleeding upon the bags of grain. It does seem very different indeed."

"I must think upon it," he replied, lighting his pipe, "but upon another point, I believe we've made headway."

"What is that?" I asked curiously.

"Do you remember the killer's words in his first epistle Watson, specifically in regard to the place of his birth?"

"He said he passed by the old pile where he was

born almost every day, oh, and that he'd likely die near there as well."

"Yes and we know there are a great many 'old piles,' as you called it, in Whitechapel, but he used a different word for the place, if you recall. No? He called it, 'the humble ramshackle of my birth,' and doubtless that conveyed far more to my mind than he would have expected or hoped it would. An old pile, after all, may refer to a wide range of decrepit tumble-downs, but a ramshackle is a much more descriptive and limiting word. It suggests something more than merely a decrepit old place. It brought a rambling hodge-podge to my mind and after all the miles spent in Whitechapel I believe I've identified the exact place," he pronounced well-pleased with his results.

"But how did you narrow the area down?"

"Simple Watson. I reasoned that the killer would likely select places for his crimes where he was most comfortable and confident. No place would be more apt to conjure those feelings than the places he lived and worked, and the route between those two locations. So after the first killing I'd narrowed the possibilities to four. After this morning I have a much better idea and only one of those places lies near that course, at the intersection of Darling Row and Lisbon Street," said he, "and barring another murder tonight I plan to be at that spot tomorrow to see who passes by."

"Do you think there will be another, that is a murder tonight?"

"I believe that depends upon the coverage the

Langford Murder receives."

"So if there is a rousing article, his message is quoted, and he is connected to the Three Colts Killing, he'll strike again. But if he is disappointed he'll have to make more adjustments?"

"No one will connect the murders as yet. He guaranteed that when he changed his methods so radically. As to the article, it will be only a few words upon a back page."

"So you already know the reception the killing will receive?"

"I've deduced as much Watson, and as the official channels have told the City's press to avoid focusing upon the gangs, Big Pat Langford's tragic passing will not raise many eyebrows."

"So, few will be bothered by the passing of the gang leader."

"The Constant Correspondent may not have grasped how the people would react to the murder of the most dangerous and despised members of their society."

"I see, so instead of raising an army, our man may have unwittingly given London's citizens cause to celebrate?"

"I have no doubt that some will mourn the passing of Gam Tzomides and Big Pat Langford, but they will be few indeed. Even among their own men, those in line for power will be celebrating."

The post finally delivered us the envelope with the sweeping script in the late afternoon.

"It is here," I called to Holmes.

"Read it out Watson, if you will."

"Gentlemen," the third letter began, abandoning its previous form of addressing only Holmes, *"The Baker Street Boys have been naughty. You haven't been playing the straight game with me. Scratching out my messages and hiding the bodies from the good people of London, you won't see that kind of thing upon the playing fields of Eton Mr. Holmes! I wonder if you've realized that you're playing a losing game yet or if you really think you will be able to foil me throughout. Two devils down and you're still no closer to discovering who your foeman is. That will never do.*

You have been busy though and I've watched you going about your business with a purpose. I have to admire energy even when it is put into a losing effort, but by now you must have learned that I am hard to predict.

You cannot keep London quiet much longer although why you even try Mr. Holmes, is a puzzle. Why defend those who ridicule you? You need not remain the laquais of the Yard forever."[14]

Only five more dead men between me and the good doctor. Your Obedient Servant, The Constant Correspondent."

"Why does he sign his letters, 'Your Obedient Servant' Holmes?"

"For the same reason he calls me a Scotland Yard stooge and lackey Watson, to mock me."

---

[14] "Laquais" the French from which the archaic British English word "lacquey" comes, itself the root from which the modern "lackey" is derived. A mindless and servile worker, especially for someone in a position of higher rank.

"But he's said that you are the only one worthy to be his foeman."

"Then look at it like this," Holmes replied, "he does it to emphasize that I have no power over him."

"And yet you still consider him balanced?"

"I begin to wonder. This case is proving deeper and more challenging than I at first judged. While I reconsider my ideas I await the next murder as it will provide me a weight of evidence which may clarify matters."

I'd seen Holmes tested many times but rarely had I seen him unsure of himself for long. He'd identified our killer as a lithe, strong man between 27 and 32, traveling with a carrying case. The man had smooth-soled dress shoes of a clerk or teller, a long, lightweight raincoat of dark Continental Blue, was five feet seven inches tall, with dark brown mid-length hair, and a bandaged left hand. Now however, he seemed troubled.

When our first paper arrived that evening I scanned the front page for the story on the murder of the Irish gang boss in Whitechapel but there was nothing. Again and again, page by page, there was nothing. Then on page six, near the bottom of the page was a short article under the heading "Montague Street Murder."

"Here it is Holmes," I exclaimed, "page six under the title 'Montague Street Murder.'" said I excitedly. "An official source confirmed that a man by the name of Patrick Seamus Langford, believed a member of a criminal gang, was shot in front of a grain warehouse on Old Montague Street at 4:45 this morning in what was described as a 'retribution killing' by another gang. The presence of a religious quote upon the wall was put down to an effort to throw Police off the scent of the true murderer. This reporter was assured that the trick will not fool our men in uniform."

"That's it?" Holmes asked.

"That's everything."

"Oh Watson," said he, the dread clear in his voice, "I fear the time the Inspector spoke of has come at last."

"What time is that?"

"Remember he said that by the time the killer reached the third murder he'd..." then Holmes went silent and I picked up.

"He'd roll the victim out right in front of the morning crowds, leaving us helpless to counter him," I said, finishing Inspector Caldecott's words as precisely as I could.

"Yes," Holmes nodded. "Do you realize that the morning delivery drivers could literally do just that, roll the victim out right in front of the morning crowds that is?"

"Surely they would be aware of the dead man immediately," I said in horror at the very thought.

"Perhaps," Holmes said noncommittally, "you may be right."

"The very idea," I exclaimed, "if it were possible, it would achieve all of his hopes."

"No doubt you are right though Watson. The idea is an absurd one."

I could see that Holmes wanted to believe that the idea he'd envisioned was far-fetched but as much as he now said this, I wondered if the morning would bring just such a thing.

The thing was that Inspector Caldecott and his men were exhausted by their extra efforts and long hours. He'd had to rotate men off and had gotten little support for replacements from his superiors. As frustrating as this might seem we all understood that it was the inevitable result of his reporting, that this was not a single, deranged killer but random and unrelated crimes.

Holmes too had been pushing himself beyond what was good for him and, at least in my opinion, needed a good night's rest.

"What do you gather from the latest letter?" I asked, half in the hope of focusing my friend's mind on something other than the disturbing notion that the morning would bring a new nightmare to Whitechapel.

"I take it that the man is an outsider Watson, both by class and by sentiment. His reference in the second letter to 'as any of your class at University,' and in the third letter, to 'the playing fields of Eton,' smacks of someone who wished they'd been able to go to those kinds of schools and couldn't. His attitude to Scotland Yard, while I can sympathize as you well know, again sounds the outsider with little to lose should London ignite into what you referred to as a vigilante movement. Finally, he has been watching us, not here in Baker Street, at least not consistently, for I would have noticed and the

Irregulars would have reported it. "

"But there is nothing new in this Holmes. After all, he told us this much in his first letter. He said he had no education at all, except for what he'd given himself, and that he was born in a ramshackle in Whitechapel where he'd lived all his life."

"Yes, you are correct that he said as much, but there are two points I would bring to your attention. First, simply because he said a thing does not make it true. Would you agree?"

"Of course."

"Second, and here I ask you to answer quickly Watson and instinctively, do this man's letters sound as if they are the work of a purely self-educated man?"

"No," I declared quickly, just as Holmes had directed.

"No?"

"No!"

"But do you know why you said 'no' Watson?"

I thought about this for a moment and had to admit that, on the face of it, I did not."

"Precisely, your subconscious, when given free rein, proves the truer judge of these letters. When the conscious becomes involved it struggles to fathom what the subconscious comprehended instinctively."

"What I don't understand is, why did I say 'no' in the first place, for I tell you that I had not questioned the matter before you asked me?"

"As I too was inclined to do Watson, you aren't alone in that. I knew we would learn more about our correspondent with each new letter and each new murder. It also holds that he would exercise more care to mask his first letter than he would for any subsequent one, just as he took such cares to stage and prepare that first murder. With each next step we saw more deeply into the man and that was one of the reasons for my puzzlement."

"What was that Holmes?"

"I'll ask you again Watson, to answer quickly and instinctively. From the start, did you take this man to be a Frenchman?"

"No," I exclaimed quickly, then I added, "he said himself that he'd been born in Whitechapel."

"Yes, he did say that."

"But as you pointed out, simply because he said a thing does not make it true."

"Now you begin to see and just as the second murder was committed with a French-made pistol and the third letter introduced the use of the French word for 'lacquey.' 'You need not remain the laquais of the Yard forever.' Surely Watson, a self-educated Englishman would have used the classic spelling, 'lacquey,' or the emerging form of 'lackey,' would he not."

"He could have purchased the pistol in any shop in Whitechapel, or on the street even, don't you agree Holmes? Don't you think you may be trying to read too much into the thing?"

"Do you know how many of the LeMat revolvers were produced Watson?"

"I'm afraid..."

"Yes," he replied curtly, "During the same period that saw the production of nearly a hundred-thousand Enfield revolvers here at home, the total number of LeMat's manufactured between Liège, Belgium, and Paris, France, totalled only 2,700. Of that number 900 went to the Confederate Army, 600 went to the Confederate Navy and 500 went to the Confederate Capitol in Richmond, Virginia."

"Leaving only 700 to be dispersed elsewhere," I said quietly, in admission that purchasing such a weapon in Whitechapel, of all places, was the extreme of longshots.

"It is the simplest of mathematical calculations my dear fellow. You stand three times the chance of being struck down by a lightning bolt while walking out upon Hampstead Heath than you do of finding a LeMat in Whitechapel and just about even odds of finding one in a London shop."

"As to a self-educated Whitechapel man using words like 'lacquey,' it runs counter what we can reliably hypothesize."

"So that's why you said this case had difficulties."

"Yes, in part."

"Well then, I have to tell you something that may increase those difficulties," I said nervously, for I knew how much my friend counted on me and I hated to fail him. "I told you I'd seen no one in the crowd Holmes, and as far as that goes it's true, for I failed to get any kind of real look at the man who turned away. Dark, top hat, black coat, moving quickly away from me, that was all."

"Well, we had one chance Watson and that was

it," Holmes said dryly, "he surely won't make that mistake a second time. All we can do is pick up tomorrow as best we can. For now my dear fellow, you will be glad to know that I am off to my bed."

"And you won't rise and slip away in the night as you are wont to do?"[15]

"I promise you," said he solemnly, "if I am away it will be because Caldecott called for me and I'll be in company with you. Does that satisfy my doctor?"

"Quite," I said, pleased to know he would finally give his body the rest it required.

It was nearly nine the next morning when the Police carriage pulled to a quick stop in front of our door and Inspector Caldecott leapt out.

"He looks frantic Watson," Holmes noted as we heard the man come through the door and bound up several steps at a time until he stood before us, red-faced and panting.

"It's a nightmare Mr. Holmes!" he gasped and then collapsed upon the old Persian carpet.

We laid the man upon the settee and I gave him a glass of water mixed with a diluted sedative. It would calm him but little more.

"Take your time Inspector," Holmes said with a kindly smile.

"Time!" the man erupted. "We have no time."

"Whatever it is, there is little we can do now," Holmes reasoned logically.

"You must remain calm Inspector Caldecott," I insisted as I placed a wet cloth upon his forehead.

---

[15] "wont to do" – accustomed to do.

"Take your time Inspector," Holmes said again in his kindest voice, "and tell us everything in its turn. Leave nothing out."

The poor man tried to sit up and I propped him on several pillows.

"I was called out at half-five. Everything had been quiet until then Mr. Holmes, a strangely quiet night really," he noted and then paused to take his drink.

"Where were you called?"

"Tower Bridge," said he simply. "By the time I arrived crowds had already gathered and hundreds of gawkers had taken boats out upon the Thames."

We remained silent as Caldecott clearly labored to gather his wits.

"You see, a crucified man was hung from the center of the overhead cross-section which runs between the towers. He was easily 80 feet above the river and people had been gathering for some time."

"My men had blocked access to the cross-section and waited for me. When I arrived I took Dugan Gallagher, a sergeant and my most trusted man, and swore him to absolute silence, as the two of us would be the only men to see the victim initially. You know what I suspected Gentlemen, for by now I was used to our killer's signature, but nothing could have prepared me for what we saw when we pulled the man up to the walkway."

He took another drink and shook his head as if it would settle him.

"Once we got him up to us the first thing we noticed was that he was nailed through the palms, into a heavy beam which was itself affixed with all manner of metal bits and pulleys."

These words filled me with horror and I couldn't but imagine the sight that met the Inspector and the sergeant when they first laid the body upon the walkway.

"One of the workmen told me later that the beam or timber was used to suspend a platform for maintenance on the cross-section."

"So the killer had to know about it, somehow," Holmes said, "and knowing he had it to work with saved him the need to take one up with him."

"We found a blindfold and gag on the walkway, but they were subsequently lost over the side when we brought the body up. There was another message too," said he, rolling awkwardly to his side and pulling a wooden placard out from under the back of his coat. He handed it to Holmes and again leaned back upon the pillows."

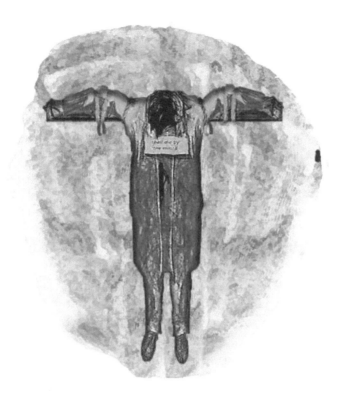

"shall die by the sword," Holmes read aloud before handing it over to me.

"From the Gospel of Matthew," I replied.

"Then said Jesus unto him, put up again thy sword into its place: for all they that take the sword shall perish by the sword,"[16] Holmes quoted.

"The man's arms were lashed to the beam as well and ropes suspended him in mid-air, arms outstretched."

---

[16] Matthew 26:52.

"He was placed so as to make it impossible to remove the body quickly, while being visible to as many passers-by as was possible," said Holmes.

"Our killer has indeed learned his lesson," I added with a sense of defeat.

"He has at that Dr. Watson," the Inspector said, "but good old Sergeant Gallagher had a brainstorm up there on that catwalk and told me to hide the placard under my coat. Then cutting the ropes and pulling the victim's hands over the nails he pushed the timber off, to be lost forever on the bottom of the Thames.

"But how has this helped us?" I pleaded. "All had seen the thing and knew."

"Not so," the Inspector declared, "I have no notion what our killer was thinking. The place was certainly public, in as far as that goes, but no one below could have read the message and only the keenest eyes among them could have seen the ropes let alone the nails. In the dim light of dawn even that was questionable."

"No doubt the killer believed a large group of men would retrieve the body, perhaps even before you arrived, and every fact would be repeated to the press," Holmes offered.

"No doubt you are correct Mr. Holmes, but my men made sure that didn't happen."

"Is there anything else you consider illustrative about the Tower Bridge Killing?" Holmes asked. "And have you determined identity yet?"

"There are...difficulties with identification."

"How so Inspector?" I asked.

"Truth be told Dr. Watson and even though he was only up there for a few hours, the sea birds, well, you see."

The thought of the sea birds disfiguring the man seemed just as Inspector Caldecott described it when he first came in, a nightmare.

"His face?" I said, trying not to imagine it.

"And his hands Dr. Watson, all exposed flesh. Then too, it seems our killer has a particularly nasty side to him. After he got the victim strung up he stabbed him in his side, from below the rib cage and in an upward thrust. It seems to have been a mercy, as the victim died of blood loss long before he would have died of thirst or exposure. By the time we'd finished wrapping our man in canvas tarpaulin and got him down in the lift we'd agreed that he was a suicide victim."

"And with so much of the evidence hidden or discarded," Holmes said, "pushing that narrative became much easier. But then why did you call it a nightmare Inspector, for you have done it all rather admirably."

"It is a nightmare Mr. Holmes," the man cried out, nearly hysterical again.

"Calm yourself Inspector, remember your men are counting on you."

"As our we Inspector Caldecott," Holmes said, "so steady on and explain yourself."

"It was the other killing Mr. Holmes, the man hanging in St. Mary's Church on Whitechapel High Street. We didn't learn of it until we'd come down from the bridge."

"A second murder on the same night?" I cried, horrified that our situation was now spinning out of control.

"So that was his plan," Holmes said in little more than a whisper.

"Hundreds had crowded into the church by the

time we arrived and he hung close to the people."

"Close enough to read the killer's message I'm guessing."

"That's right Dr. Watson. Close enough to read the 'Judas' placard and to recognize the man even through the lacerations on the face."

"Judas, a betrayer and traitor," Holmes added.

"And who was he?" I asked.

"Fitzhugh Pomeroy, Dr. Watson."

"I remember him," said I, "what was it, a year ago Holmes?"

"About that Watson but he got off rather quickly didn't he Inspector."

"A technicality," the Inspector said, hanging his head, "but everyone knew he was guilty."

"That's why the killer finds it so easy to blame our legal system for its bungling and ineptness," Holmes said, nodding in understanding. "And this was his effort to rectify that miscarriage."

"That being true Mr. Holmes, I guess I have a confession to make."

"I still don't know who the Tower Bridge victim is, but with Gam Tzomides being the first, Big Patrick Langford, the second, and now, this Fitzhugh Pomeroy, who poisoned and killed eleven people including his own children, and all for the money, I guess I'm beginning to pull for the killer."

"I understand your sentiments Inspector, but I must warn you most solemnly not to make them known outside this room. You would find the world to be much less understanding than Dr. John Watson and Mr. Sherlock Holmes."

Chapter 5 – The Indomitable Inspector Caldecott

After the Inspector departed, feeling much better, Holmes soon limped out in the disguise of a weather-beaten beggar.

"I will return in the evening Watson," said he from the stairs.

He had mastered the art of disguises to a point that he would have been a marvel upon the stage in London, New York, or Paris. His thespian powers never ceased to amaze and his mastery of the various accents alive across the country meant that he could venture in freely among the people nearly anywhere.

We didn't know if or when we'd receive a letter from the Constant Correspondent but Holmes couldn't wait any longer to be out upon the trail.

Only one paper had managed to get a story of the Tower Bridge incident in their morning edition. As the victim had gotten the attention of thousands of Londoners and even in boats upon the Thames, the paper granted it a front-page billing with a vivid illustration. The banner headline, however, would not please our Constant Correspondent. Thanks to the brilliance of Sergeant Dugan Gallagher and the indomitable Inspector Caldecott, the case had been accepted as a suicide. The papers seemed almost as happy to accept the story as were the Inspector's Scotland Yard superiors.

"Tragic Suicide Shakes Tower Bridge," ran in

The Morning Post and outsold all other papers combined. By evening every paper was running the story.

As to the murdered man hanging in St. Marys Church, none of the papers had time to run the story in their morning editions. The irony of all this had made it easier for London to accept the Tower Bridge Suicide since the identity of the man was not known, whereas the murder of the man in St. Marys Church seemed of little concern once it was disclosed that the dead man was the mad poisoner of nearly a dozen people including his own small children, Fitzhugh Pomeroy, who'd gotten off on a technicality.

When the papers did run the story it was at the bottom of the second page under a variety of unsympathetic titles similar to that of The Times, which read, "Murderer is himself Murdered." It was early evening when the Inspector arrived.

"You've done remarkably Inspector," I said, "for no one as yet suspects that all these killings are the work of one man."

"I've been guided by Mr. Holmes from the start," he replied modestly. "I've also had the help of several good men like Sergeant Gallagher. I'll entrust you with a secret Dr. Watson," said he, "that one of my allies is our acting coroner."[17]

---

[17] All violent deaths were supposed to have a post-mortem but a severe shortage of coroners in England during the period made such a goal impossible. Meanwhile post-mortems of suicides were notoriously hit-and-miss and varied widely by location.

"I wondered how you were managing."

"That's our secret mind you," he said, tapping the side of his nose with his index finger.

I nodded in silent agreement.

"Now, as Mr. Holmes isn't yet in I'll leave you with the identity of the Tower Bridge victim and you can pass it along."

With that he gave me a name that sent chills up my spine, for Abraham Stibbe, better known as Bram the Beast, was the chief muscle for the Irish McAuley Gang which had been led until recently by Big Pat Langford. It was widely believed that Stibbe had killed and beaten more men in London than any other man, but the Police could never get a thing on him. He had also been the Whitechapel "collector" for all the protection money paid by out by the businesses.

"The McAuley's must be feeling the heat," I remarked, "as two of their top men have been taken out within days of each other."

"And to think that Bram the Beast's death has gone down as a suicide, that alone would make him roll over in his grave. I'm beginning to feel a strong appreciation for this Constant Correspondent and though I say it myself Dr. Watson, my men are unusually pleased that we haven't succeeded in collaring this killer. As long as he keeps killing the worst of the devils we've had to deal with all these years, I think they'd be happy to keep looking the other way."

Source "Death's Gatekeepers: The Victorian Coroner's Office" by C. Watson, ©2016, legalhistorymiscellany.com.

I understood the Inspector's sentiment although it shocked me to hear a man of his standing say it. The truth was I suspected Holmes himself of feeling the same "appreciation" for our correspondent.

"So do I rightly gather, Inspector, that you think this Constant Correspondent is an altogether sane man."

"I'm no specialist, if that's what you mean," said he, "but I don't think any truly sane man would dare go after the most dangerous men in London. I know if I were tasked with that job I'd fairly blanch at the mere thought of it. You have to remember that we estimated Bram Stibbe's murder total at close on a hundred men, many of them Whitechapel business owners, but your Correspondent nailed that devil's hands to a beam, stuck him in the side like the Roman Centurion did to the Lord, then hung him out on the Tower Bridge for everyone to see. Like an advertisement it was!"

"Have you had a chance to read Stevenson's new book?" I asked to all appearances changing the subject.

"That's the one about the man who turns into a monster is it? No, I have little time to partake of such enjoyments Dr. Watson, mores the pity, for I tend to spend most of my waking hours chasing real monsters. I think that's why so many of the boys are inclined to view your Constant Correspondent as a champion of the people, like I said before. He's actually hunting the monsters and you'd be mistaken if you didn't think the monsters still alive weren't more than a little scared."

"The reason I ask is," I explained, "that in the book Dr. Jekyll is a good man but deep inside of him lives this other part, whom Stevenson identifies as Mr. Hyde."

"So it's Mr. Hyde who does all the dirty work?"

"That's right and I've been wondering if our killer might be a real-life Jekyll & Hyde."

""He could be. A decent bloke by day, going about a regular life, working hard, living, but always watching the devils literally get away with bloody murder. Then, at night he becomes the hunter, prowling the streets and alleys looking for his prey."

"Right, something like that," I said.

Holmes walked in just then, removing his well-worn disguise even as he stood looking at us.

"Any letter yet Watson?" he called out.

"No, but Inspector Caldecott has the identity of the Tower Bridge victim."

"Bram Stibbe!" said Holmes frankly.

"How the devil did you know that Mr. Holmes?"

"Your man showed me the body, that tattoo Inspector. After all it's not every day that the son of a Jewish father and an Irish Catholic mother takes up the vocation of cold-blooded killer is it?"

"You are a wonder Mr. Holmes, there is no doubt about that."

"What was this tattoo?" I enquired.

"Bram Stibbe had a truly original tattoo upon his chest Dr. Watson. You might even say that he was known for it, among his other accomplishments that is," the Inspector smiled. "It was an amalgam really, a Jewish Menorah forming the crossbeam on a

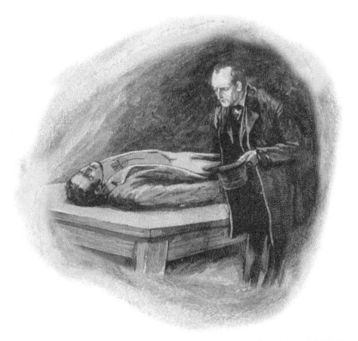

Christian Cross, surmounted with the initials, INRI. He boasted that the thing made him bullet-proof."

"INRI?" I repeated, "Jesus the Nazarene, King of the Jews."[18]

"That's right Dr. Watson. Bram Stibbe was a devotee, of sorts."

This revelation left me quite stunned as how a brutal killer could find any solace in either of the classic religions was utterly beyond my grasp.

"Well," said Holmes, handing me an envelope with the now chillingly familiar sweeping script. "What do you think of that Watson?"

---

[18] "IESVS·NAZARENVS·REX·IVDAORVM" in Latin. There were no letters 'J' of 'U' in the language at that time.

"Did you get the post?" I exclaimed, for I'd not heard it arrive.

"No, although I expect our letter at any moment. No, this is something very different. Do you recall I have several men working at the papers?"

"Of course," I said, "but I've not heard you refer to them in some time."

"Well, I gave our envelopes to my people at The Times, The Morning Post, and The Illustrated Police News and told them to watch for an envelope with the same sweeping script."

"You knew the killer couldn't help himself. If we continued to foil him, you knew that at some point he'd have to communicate directly with one of the papers and you preempted him Mr. Holmes."

The Inspector was beside himself with respect and admiration for Holmes and I too was amazed at my friend's astuteness.

"Go ahead Watson, read it out," said he, taking his place in his chair and stretching his long, thin legs out.

"To the Editor of The Times, This letter is to inform you that I am the murderer of the four criminals who have recently met their deaths, Gamaliel Tzomides, a known extortionist and practiced beater-of-women, Patrick Langford, the leader of the McAuley Gang and a chief promoter of all manner of evil, Abraham Stibbe, a brutal killer of many of my Whitechapel friends and neighbors, and Fitzhugh Pomeroy, the infamous poisoner. All of these men were protected by the Police and even now forces are working to obscure the facts. Before

*I have run my course I will kill three more criminals
whom law enforcement has allowed to walk free.
Now that you know the truth you must tell all the
world. Otherwise you are á contre-sens and the
equivalent of a conspirator with these criminals.
The Concerned Citizen."*

"Did you notice," the Inspector said, "that in the
letters he sends you and in this letter, he signs
himself with two words starting in 'C'? The Constant
Correspondent and The Concerned Citizen."

"That is an interesting observation," Holmes
agreed.

"And what is this French phrase at the end?" I
asked, "I'm not familiar with it."

"That is an odd ending Watson and it doesn't
have an exact translation. Used here I would say it
means that unless the Editor publishes the facts as
the Concerned Citizen sees them, then he is going
about his job 'in the wrong way.'"

"What will you do with that letter Mr. Holmes,
for I take it you won't give it to the Editor."

"No," Holmes replied with a satisfied smile.
"I've already ordered a few lines in the personals
which starts, 'To The Concerned Citizen,' and says,
basically, 'we are not interested in your information
so stop wasting our time.' It is signed 'TE.'"

"'TE' for 'The Editor, that is very clever Mr.
Holmes, but it will be sure to anger him. No doubt
he'll reach out to the other papers but as you've
already gotten men posted at the leading ones
perhaps he will be stymied long enough to keep the
lid on this thing. I feel we've been lucky so far,

although a part of me wonders why we're fighting this. No offense Dr. Watson, I understand that he's threatened your life, I only mean..."

"It's alright Inspector, you have enough on your shoulders without worrying about my feelings."

It was said nobly, but my fears were real and as Inspector Caldecott had pointed out, this man, whoever he was, wasn't afraid to hunt the most dangerous men in London. Next to the likes of Bram Stibbe and Big Pat Langford, who was Dr. John Watson?

"I say we've cornered the man and foiled him at almost every step," Holmes pronounced, "but the truth is, Inspector, that you and your men have done all the heavy lifting to this point."

These words struck Inspector Caldecott very much by surprise and to receive the open praises of Sherlock Holmes was rare indeed.

"I'm not sure what to say Mr. Holmes, but I will see that my men hear of your tribute."

"And on that note Inspector, as he has been so thoroughly obstructed thus far, we have now seen him literally double his efforts with two murders. As you pointed out, when he sees the words in the personal adds it will likely infuriate him. Silence and distortions from the papers regarding his murders, such as the 'suicide' of Bram Stibbe, will push him to even more radical action."

"Holmes," I declared, "we've already seen one man crucified upon a gate, one with his hands nailed to a beam and suspended from Tower Bridge, one killed with a highly unusual revolver, and yet another hanging from the rafters in St. Marys Church. After all that how much more radical can he be?"

It was then we heard the characteristic "clink" of the brass cover of our mail slot.

"I was hoping very much that the letter would arrive before I left," the Inspector confessed, "and now the mail has come."

"Is it there Watson?"

"It is," I muttered as I went through the stack. "That sweeping cursive is here."

I took it to my chair and sat deliberately down, the way a man does when he has a serious task before him.

"Mr. Holmes," I began as usual, *"for a man of utter insignificance and no education to speak of, I have certainly given our City something to talk about and to be grateful for, have I not? Four devils down and even you must admit that the world becomes a better place every day I'm about my business. If you were willing to be honest about our little game, you'd realize that I've done more good in one week than you have in as many years. You see, though the world hangs upon your every word and pays me no attention at all, I want the great detective to understand a simple principle. Justice must be done Mr. Holmes. I believe you've forgotten this, but I am a good teacher and there is no arguing with this truth. Justice is to a nation what flour is to a baker. If you have it you may succeed, with hard work, but if you don't, then there is simply no hope for you. Rome is the ultimate example but the Empire*

rushes, even now, to fall as well. It is an absolute truth and the nation which ceases to deliver justice will soon be replaced by another. Mark my word. History proves it. In fact, although I never sat in any of your fine classrooms worrying over your myriad exams, and never tested my mettle upon your hallowed fields and tracks, I will instruct the great man. The undercutting of a nation's system of justice is the surest way to destroy it. Justice must be done and it must be seen to be done! This is what I am doing, day by day, while you merely chase me like a dog chasing its own tail.

If you or that Scotland Yard drone of yours, Caldecott, were honorable men you'd realize that I am not your enemy nor am I England's enemy. In fact, how many of those do-nothings at the Yard or in our government are greater threats to English Justice than your obedient servant? Think upon it Mr. Holmes, but a little longer. CC"

"The man has no concept of a paragraph," I muttered to myself.

"And he feels no remorse for his actions either," Holmes added.

"Yet he is onto something there Mr. Holmes you must admit, for even among the roughs we've heard grumblings and fear."

"It doesn't take the rats long to sense a sinking ship," Holmes admitted, "yet the lack of any kind of regret upon the part of the killer is...instructive, is it not?"

"How so?" asked the Inspector. "For we know he feels only hatred for these creatures, as many among us do."

"No doubt you're correct Inspector," Holmes agreed, "I only point out that he resents me for my education and position in society, he despises you for your place at the Yard, and he has threatened Dr. Watson's life despite our friend's innocence in every regard. Surely this man must view himself as wronged by the whole world."

"I see your point Holmes," I replied, "but surely anyone who could accuse the Inspector of being a mindless drone, blindly following the directives of the Yard, is a man utterly out of touch with reality. For even this case itself argues most strongly against such a judgment."

"Thank you Dr. Watson, it is always encouraging when someone else sees things as I do. If this man could see how I've endangered my career he'd soon recant his words wouldn't he?"

"Excellent Watson," said he, "That too is illustrative is it not, that he shows an utter ignorance of the realities at the Yard."

"As with you Holmes," I pointed out, "for all of his talk of about the hallowed halls of fine schools he knows nothing in fact, apparently at least, of the years you spent learning from private tutors."

"You are quite correct Watson. I suppose both Mycroft and I were something of a challenge to educate and there has never been any attempt to hide that fact."

"So, although he pretends to be knowledgeable of these things, are we saying that he's actually quite out of touch with things?"

"That is very well-said Inspector, quite out of touch save in regard to the criminal classes of Whitechapel, of whom he seems quite conversant and familiar."

"And what does that convey Holmes?"

"Alone it is a mere point, an observation, which could present little that is helpful. Taken with other evidence Watson, it may yet prove to be supremely revealing."

"Well, as much as I praise the man's judgment and effort thus far and in private, I understand where you are coming from Mr. Holmes."

"Indeed and where is that Inspector," I replied, "for I am still a bit in the fog in that direction."

"Only that in the current instance, with these four swings, your Correspondent has clipped all the right geese, what of his threats toward you? I've never known a more honorable man than you Dr. Watson and many of my fellows would agree most soundly with that, you can be sure!"

To say that these words didn't nearly unsettle me would be a lie for seldom had anyone ever declared my virtue more stoutly or concisely. It reminded me that while we may have even daily interaction with some, we rarely discern their true opinions of us.

"And innocent of any crime," he continued, "most certainly. So while saluting his initial efforts it simply will not do having every citizen feeling themselves free to wreak their own vengeance upon any they would like. Can you imagine such a world, when even an innocent man like you Doctor, is subjected to the threat of death?"

"I must salute you Inspector, for you have captured my view completely. As poorly as the structures of society sometimes operate and as easy a target as they may provide critics such as myself and our Constant Correspondent, wanton anarchy would soon see a return to the lawlessness of, say, America's wild west. You may recall, Inspector, the case of the 'Study in Scarlet' which occurred in 1881 and in which the men Drebber and Stangerson were both murdered."

I remember it well Mr. Holmes and I might add that the case went a long way in establishing your reputation at the Yard."

Holmes nodded appreciatively but made no comment as to the kind remark.

"That case is a good example of how personal notions of revenge or justice can come to unleash havoc among an altogether innocent society. Both Drebber and Stangerson were Americans and Mormons, from Salt Lake City. Jefferson Hope, another American, was their pursuer and had vowed to get his revenge upon them. They fled to Europe and ultimately washed up here in London, where Hope came upon them and fulfilled his vow. So it was that some misfortune a half-a-world away became a tragedy in our metropolis."

"I remember that Hope died just before his own trial and I've always wondered if he had taken one of the poisoned pills he'd forced upon Enoch Drebber. Would you know anything about that?"

"If such were the case," Holmes said evasively, "then we were at least freed from enacting the final chapter in a drama of individual justice where both of the victims and the killer, as well as the cause of the trouble, were from another nation entirely."

"I see," the Inspector answered, having read in my friend's response that Holmes had indeed known about the presence of a poison pill. "The whole idea that an aneurysm would take him upon the very eve of his trial, that always struck me as a longshot simply too hard for my simple brain to believe."

"A mathematical impossibility even if distributed over a hundred thousand cases, but so few think in terms of mathematics," Holmes agreed.

"And yet there it was," the Inspector laughed, "and Gregson and Lestrade both standing there with their mouths open, looking at each other. You are a crafty customer Mr. Holmes."

"As are you Inspector Caldecott, for no one else in all these years has once questioned the death of Jefferson Hope upon the night before his trial was to begin. I find that as a species we are among the most accepting of all the animals. I thought it likely that the man who killed with a poisoned pill might have kept one back for just such a possibility and, considering it but a small mercy, I said nothing of what I suspected."

Chapter 6 – The Face of Mr. Hyde

I slept fitfully and finally gave it up, rising early despite my weariness. I lit the fire then stretched and opened the curtain to the dim gray of a London sunrise blanketed in fog.

When I did my eyes immediately fell upon a huge crowd filling Baker Street. At such an hour it was unheard of and it took my poor eyes a moment to see what they were all looking at, as the buildings opposite were upon the darker side of the street and a thick fog was rolling in. Then my eyes caught site of something that made my heart stop.

My friend, Mr. Sherlock Holmes, hung dead upon the far side of Baker Street, his arms stretched out in the shape of a cross and suspended by rope. His head was hanging down as if he were imparting some great wisdom to the crowd below but the skin was a dead, cold gray.

I've no idea how long I stood staring there at the window but the next moment I was conscious of many in the street had turned and were looking at me. My mind was suddenly alive and I ran to Holmes' bedroom even though I knew I would find it empty and the bed as cold as the man. I flung the door open with a great slam and was several feet into the room before I realized that Sherlock Holmes was staring at me from his bed, with the most puzzled look upon his face.

"Watson?" said he, groggily.

I pulled the startled man from his bed in his nightshirt and gave him no opportunity to even put his slippers upon his bare feet. I rushed with him through the sitting room and stood him before the window.

To my amazement and upon seeing Holmes the crowd began clapping and then, slowly, they began to cheer. Soon hats were tossed in the air and the hoorahs and the huzzahs interrupted the sleep of confused neighbors up and down Baker Street. It was clear that the crowd had thought just as I had, that the man hanging upon the building opposite 221B was Mr. Sherlock Holmes himself.

They didn't disperse until more police arrived to augment the poor chap who'd so bravely stood his ground. Even then a hardy dozen or two remained, curious to see what was yet to come.

Holmes said little but nodded to the crowd and turning, whispered to me.

"No doubt Watson, our killer was somewhere in that crowd or nearby, watching us."

Time and time again Holmes had told me that people see the form but they do not observe the details. I had just been given the perfect lesson of that. I had watched the crowd for several minutes and could describe only its general size and mood and nothing of the details. Holmes words mobilized my mind but too late, as most of the crowd was turned away south toward Marylebone Road and the bulk of the jobs. My eyes now searched the few faces still turned up at our window, but I was too late.

"Who is he?" I asked, a half hour later and in the empty rooms in the flat opposite.

"Gentleman Dick Lanier, boss of the Redmen," Inspector Caldecott said, "on account of their home territory being on Redman Road, over toward Stepney."

"Was he killed here?" I asked, looking around the dark room lit by one lantern.

"He was taken from his coach last night at gunpoint, but I doubt we'll ever know where he was killed. No blood though, not to speak of, so he was dead before they got here."

As I thought of the man hanging just beyond the window, whose lifeless gray hand I could just see, with the rope that held it, I thought to myself that I was looking into the face of Stevenson's Mr. Hyde. The man who could do all of this was himself a monster.

"He was carried up the back stairs and brought in here," Holmes said upon his return to the rooms. "All the knots used were common, square nots and half-hitches."

"So our Correspondent isn't a sailor."

"That's right Inspector, but as you've pointed out, he's a bold one and unafraid of taking even the most dangerous. Gentleman Dick was a foremost scuttler Watson."

"As in a sinker of ships?"

"As in a street brawler," the Inspector clarified, "pick your weapon, knife, club, hatchet, axe, chain, or pistol, he was your man. That's how he got to the top of the pile among the Redmen."

Several policemen brought the body in through one of the windows and laid it down on the floor where, in the dim lantern light and the faint light now entering through the windows, Holmes conducted his impromptu postmortem.

"He was struck on the head," said he. "The blow would've proven fatal itself with time but again we see the knife wound in the side, just as with the Tower Bridge Murder. That had the effect of speeding things up significantly," he muttered. "Now this is of interest," he continued, moving the victim's hand into the lantern light. "Do you see that Gentlemen?"

"What? His fingernails," asked the Inspector.

"It is gray," said I, "under the fingernails, almost blue Holmes."

"Almost blue, that is a most significant remark Watson. Almost blue."

After a long silence during which he continued to examine the body and clothing he sat up upon his knees and looked at us.

"Gentleman Dick Lanier, the late boss of the Redmen, was killed in Flower & Dean Street," Holmes said, astonishing not only us but the four constables waiting with us to remove the body.

"Thank you Gentlemen," Holmes said as they lifted the body and disappeared out the narrow door.

"Flower & Dean aye. That makes sense Mr. Holmes for that is a haunt of vice if ever there was one. Our men dare not go there save two-by-two for there are some of the worst cutthroats in London live upon that street and in that hive."

"There are thirty-one tenement buildings along the short distance of Flower & Dean Street Inspector, more than any other street in London, and I suspect our man was killed in the alley or court of one of them."[19]

"Because of the soil under the fingernails?" I asked.

"Indeed Watson, you'll search the entire East End in vain looking for another spot with that bluish soil, very characteristic that. I discuss this very characteristic in my monograph upon the soils and substrates of London," said he casually. "Not that the place of death matters to the law courts in this case, but if it can be located it may provide some additional clues."

"You know Inspector," I remarked, "when I first looked upon the man hanging upon the wall I thought it was Holmes himself."

"As did I, Dr. Watson, I assure you. Had it not been for one of my constables, who told me that you gentlemen were waiting up here, I would have sworn to it."

"You may have noted the similar forehead and hairline," Holmes replied, "and in my old, worsted wool suit it..."

"What?" I exclaimed, interrupting my friend just a second before the Inspector would have done.

"Yes," Holmes admitted, "he was wearing the old brown suit Watson, you recall it, with the shiny knees and elbows?"

---

[19] "In Strange Company" by James Greenwood, pub. King & Co. 12 Paternoster Road, London, England, ©1873.

"Indeed," I replied, "but how Holmes?"

"Two months ago Mrs. Hudson was pestered by a charities man seeking gentlemen's throw-off suits and coats and he promised to come round again to check if she had anything. I gave her the old suit, whose better days were well behind it, and she, no doubt, handed it over to the man."

"Mr. Holmes, are you honestly implying that our killer stood upon the step at 221B Baker Street two months ago, in conversation with your landlady, and was already planning a use for your suit?"

"I see no other feasible scenarios by which Gentleman Dick Lanier might have come by my suit and upon the night of his death no less, Inspector Caldecott."

"You astonish me again Mr. Holmes but pray tell why it was so important to get the suit in the first place."

"You are staring the answer directly in the face Inspector," Holmes said as he stepped across to the window and gestured to our flat.

"Do you mean he meant for you to look upon your own death, as it were, from our very windows?"

"And that he was planning all this months ago?"

"The first point which is instructive is the pains to which the Constant Correspondent goes to in order to arrange his murders. Think about the crucifixion of Gam Tzomides."

"You called it a masterpiece Holmes."

"Indeed, Watson, and if it had been allowed to see the light of day and make the papers, there is no doubt that it would have inflamed the entire city if not the nation."

"Yes Mr. Holmes, but there was none of that with the murder of Big Pat Langford."

"Right you are Inspector and for the good reason that the boss of the McAuley's had no intention of going off quietly with his killer."

"You mean he resisted?"

"You saw for yourself, the pistol in the right hand was his calling card. While outsiders wondered at the pretentious stance of the gang leader, with his hand in his vest like a Whitechapel Napoleon, his men knew he was always ready for trouble."

"So the Constant Correspondent didn't mean to kill him in front of the grain warehouse," I said, realizing the truth of the matter for the first time.

"And no doubt our killer never intended to use the LeMat Revolver to kill the man. Every weapon a man uses, after all, provides more clues as to the man himself. Have you noticed that every other killing is accomplished silently or nearly so, and is arranged in the most dramatic of ways?"

"They are almost theatrical in their arrangement Holmes, now that you mention it."

At these words my friend stared at me hard before he spoke again.

"They are indeed...theatrical. First was Gam Tzomides' crucifixion, then we must discount the setting of Big Pat Langford's murder. This however was followed by the Tower Murder of Bram Stibbe..."

"Which couldn't have been more dramatic than it was Mr. Holmes."

"Quite right Inspector, but immediately after that, on the same night in fact, we have the body of the despised Fitzhugh Pomeroy hung grotesquely in the very sanctuary of St. Marys Church."

"And now this, another strange crucifixion directly across from our residence and with a man dressed in your own clothes," I noted.

"And did you see how he tied the body around the chest, biceps, and wrists, and all with one rope? There was some care put to that. So, are you saying that this killer was making his plans two months ago Mr. Holmes?"

"Dick Lanier was victim number five Inspector. He was preceded by Gam Tzomides, Pat Langford, Abraham Stibbe, and Fitzhugh Pomeroy. From this I take it that the planning of the first four murders was already complete by the time our killer turned to the planning of Dick Lanier's demise and thus, his need for my suit of clothes. As I said Gentlemen, the Constant Correspondent is a true technician."

"Well Mr. Holmes, this time there is nothing I can do to shield the truth of this killing. I'm afraid we'll read about this in the evening press."

"You speak as a man with the inner knowledge of these crimes Inspector. Remember that all of London believes Bram Stibbe committed suicide. Big Pat Langford was put down to a dispute over gang territory. Gam Tzomides was a simple murder at night in Whitechapel, a strangulation with a hemp rope, one inch in diameter. You and your men were able to erase or minimize the exposure of all of the religious messages from these murders. Fitzhugh

Pomeroy, the notorious poisoner, is problematic not only for his location but also for the hanging. Yet, the placard around his neck was not removed, while you'll note that this murder..."

"That's right Holmes, there was no message."

"Correct Watson, no message."

"How can that be Mr. Holmes?"

At this Holmes gave us a knowing smile and reached inside his suitcoat.

"seven deadly sins," said he, handing over a broken wooden placard with the rope still holding through one of the holes.

"What in the world is going on here?" the Inspector growled, looking around as if someone else might provide a sensible answer, but finding only us in the room.

"No doubt the killer placed this placard around the victim's neck, just as he did with Bram Stibbe and Fitzhugh Pomeroy. Placing this man's body outside the two windows presented much more of a challenge and in the process the placard was split along its length, resulting in the freeing of one end of the rope from its hole. The placard then fell by its own weight."

"Wouldn't he have noticed it?" the Inspector asked, confused.

"Remember, he came by the back stair, where a horse and cart waited for him. If he returned to the scene and mingled among the crowd he would have noticed it and been in disbelief, but by that time it was too late for him."

"And where did you find it Holmes and how?"

"Now there Watson you've gone and asked the most elementary of questions. When our man murdered his first victim, Tzomides, he painted his message upon the gate. This presented no difficulty for him as the area was remote and little traveled. When he killed Langford it was painted upon the wall again but as we now know that he was forced to rely upon the gun to neutralize his man, the loud explosion meant his message had to be rushed."

"But then he left that method behind and started using the placards."

"That's correct Inspector. This was just one of the adjustments your actions forced upon the Constant Correspondent. To place his victims in more frequented areas he couldn't afford the time it took to paint the message in situ. He also realized that carrying the case with him afforded us another means of identifying him. The use of the placards resolved both issues. As you've seen the placards can be easily hidden in a suit coat, as you did at the Tower Bridge Inspector, and as I did here in the dim hours of the morning as we came through the crowd Watson. I expected a placard and saw none, so where had it gone? It was a simple deduction and when I saw it lying in the gutter, broken and thankfully face down, it was the work of a moment to retrieve and hide it. Even you didn't notice Watson."

"That's true enough Holmes," I admitted.

"The placard had the added benefit that it could be painted days in advance and be carried dry. As he adjusted his plans to the positioning of his victims to harder to reach areas, thus giving crowds more time to see and gather, the placards were perfect. Although, as you pointed out Inspector, it was useless upon Bram Stibbe on the Tower Bridge as it was simply too far away to be seen."

"So, the seven deadly sins must refer to Dick Lanier's many crimes Mr. Holmes. Although in his case the killer could have given a much higher number, for Lanier was pure evil, distilled down."

"I understand your point Inspector, but won't these men, Lanier, Stibbe, and Langford, simply be replaced by their gangs and go on?"

"If all criminals were created equally, as our American brothers insist for the rest of humanity, then I'd agree with you most heartily Dr. Watson. But this is where this killer never ceases to amaze me Mr. Holmes, for it is as if he is handpicking the very worst devils from each area of Whitechapel. You see Doctor, these men were the Rembrandt's and Michelangelo's of crime in our city. Bram Stibbe had killed more men, by my reckoning, than the next ten most productive killers I know of."

"Indeed Inspector," Holmes replied, "and I have no doubt that our Constant Correspondent has done just as you've imagined. I believe he knows Whitechapel well. Remember he said all of his victims would be men he knew, personally. No doubt he selected the worst men he knew and these were the ones he planned for elimination. As to your concern over the papers putting two-and-two together, with the broken placard I believe we've once again foiled our killer."

"But are we getting any closer to identifying him Holmes, for as I see it he continues to operate as freely as the wind."

"And Gentleman Dick Lanier was number five Mr. Holmes, the Doctor makes a good point."

Holmes still stood at the window, looking across at our flat and down upon Baker Street as the sun began burning off the morning fog. He stared and said nothing a moment longer.

"This case is much deeper than I originally believed it, however, if we can avoid pushing him into further adjustments Gentlemen, we are now nearly upon the point of collaring our killer."

These words stunned me. As much as I knew Holmes' penchant for keeping his information back I had never imagined he'd made such progress in the case and I looked forward to returning to 221B and asking him for more details in private.

"Do you still consider him sane?" the Inspector asked.

"Yes I do but believe me when I tell you that this fact makes our killer far more dangerous than he otherwise would be, for it is a truly brilliant and lucid mind against which we are now matched. If we are not careful he may yet slip the net and then I doubt very much if we will ever run him to earth."

"And you think he has everything planned out?" I inquired.

"Before taking a trip to the continent Watson, even the average traveler will check on the return schedule and make certain he has set aside the adequate funds for the expenditure. In the same way this man has planned everything down to the last detail, in order to carry out his threat and escape our grasp permanently. If I read this killer correctly he will not be a man on the run. He will close off his great work in such a way that he will be thought of not only as an innocent man, but as the most innocent of men."

"You make him sound a genius Holmes."

"And no doubt he is Watson, but as Inspector Caldecott has noted, this man is infinitely more."

"How so?" I asked.

"A genius will break the most complex task down into a simple process, but it doesn't hold that he can stand to look a brutal killer in the eyes and not blanch. This man has gone into the lair of the monsters and thus far he has taken five of the most dangerous of them in the entire Old Country. That is a truly rare combination Watson."

"And like I said Mr. Holmes, the devils are more than a little scared, I can tell you."

We returned to our flat and Holmes took brought out a map of Whitechapel which he pinned to a board. It was much marked on and lines and diagrams ran hither and yon upon a thick stack of papers. He had that determined air about him and I determined to leave him to his labors while I turned to my case notes.

An hour passed, then two, and still he hadn't moved. Then, without my noticing it he was standing in the window, in the sunlight, holding one of the roses from the vase upon the table.

"Tell me Watson, was Shakespeare right about the rose, would it smell just as sweet if it were called by another name?"

I leaned back in my chair, glad of the break from my work and pleased with the question for once. All too often Holmes' questions left me perplexed and humbled.

"Would a rose by any other name would smell as sweet?" I said, trying to quote Juliet's line correctly.

"Yes," said he, "say we called it 'mudge,' would it still be just as fragrant as before?"

"No doubt it would Holmes, but there would be far fewer poems written about it."

"Exactly!" he declared, as if he'd not heard a word I'd said.

"What are you saying?" I asked.

"I'm only making the point that can be a fine line between one man's idea of 'justice' and a craven excuse for personal revenge, whatever it is called."

I knew I'd have to consider these words for some time, as I often did in fact, before I could make sense of them.

"Now come over here and pull up a chair Watson, for what I have to show you may save your life and spare you an extended trip across America."

I took a seat at the table and stared down at the puzzle laid out before me.

"I take it we'll be for an American Adventure if we aren't able to take this killer."

"I feel the west would be the best place for us, at least there it would be a simple thing to identify another foreigner, don't you agree?"

This was one time when I wasn't sure if Holmes were joking or not but I could see the advantage America's western lands would provide us.

Holmes pointed out thumbtacks placed for the sites of each killing, from the first on Three Colts Lane where Gam Tzomides was crucified to the last one, on Flower & Dean Street where Gentleman Dick Lanier met his end, before the humiliation of hanging on display in Baker Street.

"All of these match with the dots on the back of the first sheet, which was the only one where the Constant Correspondent used that method. Each additional murder allowed me more clues to pinpoint where the next might occur. The only building I considered a ramshackle, which fell near the line of the murders was here," he said, pointing at the intersection of Darling Row and Lisbon Street. This is the place of his birth and with the help of the Irregulars we should be able to identify a likely suspect by evening today. The trouble with the template of dots and the map was discovering which system of linking he used for the dots and simultaneously finding the correct scale for the map. It took over a thousand attempts before I had this Watson."

"Holmes, this is incredible, even for you. Is this what you've spent your nights doing?"

"It was a near impossible challenge, which is no doubt why he gave it to me," said he, shaking his head. "That I could solve it, I hope, is a reality he never seriously entertained."

"Then this circle?"

"Casson Street, where I predict the next murder will take place. Mind you, he may move the body just as he did with what the press is calling the Tower Bridge Murder, the St. Marys Church Murder, and this latest."

"Which they'll no doubt call the Baker Street Murder.

"Exactly, but the sixth murder will take place somewhere on Casson Street.

"When?" I asked.

"In the absence of knowing I have to plan for tonight and if it doesn't happen, then every night hereafter until it does."

"And should we fail on Casson Street?"

"I'm afraid, should we fail upon Casson Street, then we will be down to our last chance in the finale on Fieldgate Street, south of Whitechapel High Street. The thing is, if there is any question about succeeding in taking our man on Casson, rather than show our hand I believe we must simply wait it out until the seventh victim. It will be dangerous though Watson. You saw what our Correspondent did to the one man who resisted him."

"Yes, he didn't hesitate and that LeMat revolver made short work even of Big Pat Langford. You know Holmes, that Casson Street is very near to Flower & Dean and just as dangerous."

Chapter 7 - The Missing Magistrate

"Was that the post Watson?"

"Indeed it was and here is that damnable cursive script again," I growled angrily.

I sat down in my chair across from Holmes and was surprised to find our daily missive surprisingly short for once.

"Well Mr. Holmes, By now you've glimpsed your own death. A frightening prospect is it not? You should see how the courage of the great men I've dispatched thus far vanishes in the face of death! Quite satisfying really, when one considers how long and how freely your system has allowed these villains to operate in our city. You who revel in the play of words, that the law is what you work with while justice is what you work for, think on that! You are now a mere simpleton working for the system and against justice, a defender of corruption."

Here I stopped and faced Holmes.

"Must I continue," I pleaded, "for it is all the most trumped-up rubbish."

"Consider that every word is one more clew in our fight against our foe Watson."

"Yes, the irony of it all is so distressing, Sir. How long has it been since you were an honorable man Sherlock Holmes and when did you fall from your high place? You and your allies in their uniforms, their fine robes, their scapulars, and ermines, merely trade upon the suffering of the people, but we are nearly finished here, just two more and then... Your Obedient Servant, The Constant Correspondent."

"He refers to Lanier when he says that you've glimpsed your own death, does he not?" I asked.

"That is how I read it as well, but that was an interesting part where he spoke of my 'allies.'"

"In their robes, their scapulars, and ermines," I

reread the line, "merely trade upon the suffering."

"Somehow he's come to the belief that I am in league with the corrupt elements within the church and the judiciary, for the scapular refers to the clergyman's vestment and the robes and ermines to the judge's."

"He's like a dog with a bone Holmes, surely, and he has no idea how many dozens of devils you've seen off the streets."

"I make no excuses for the man Watson but let us not lose sight of the fact that his complaints against corruption are at least accurate."

"But the church?" I stuttered, "as if it were in league with the likes of Lanier, Langford, Stibbe, and Company.

"When the churchman gives the sacrament to someone like Bram Stibbe, or speaks glowingly of the generosity of one of the Boss's, does he not take upon himself something of the guilt as well? At least in the mind of a romantic idealist like our Constant Correspondent?"

"Is that how you see the man?" I enquired, for Holmes had never considered my point of view, that there was a mental instability at work here.

"Undoubtedly, for as you pointed out Watson, what realist could possibly put me in league with allies in the Church, at Scotland Yard, and in the Judiciary, who are bent upon protecting criminality? It is simply an untenable position for the realist and the man with his feet firmly upon terra firma. Yet this man has managed to create, how did you say,

'the most trumped-up rubbish.' How many devils in prison today curse the name of Sherlock Holmes?

"By his frequent insults of you I put him down as a man overcome with jealousy," I said.

"Now that is an astute observation indeed, and odd in one so young, is it not Watson."

Before I could answer or even bask momentarily in the compliment, he rose.

"We should leave after dark," said he, turning to the window and picking up his violin, "and you'll want to bring your revolver Watson."

"Indeed I will," said I, "and I vow not to hesitate should the situation call for action."

"I'm pleased to hear it my good fellow, for I tell you that our man will not tarry even a moment. The lesson of Big Pat Langford must not be wasted upon us Watson."

For an hour I enjoyed the most moving music imaginable and all without any breaks between. As I had found that it might be weeks between what I called my little symphonia's, I had come to value them all the more. And then it was over.

"What's this then?" Holmes said curiously, stepping nearer the window. "A veiled lady in sateen stepping down from one of London's commonest Hansom's. That will never do."

He put his violin away and checked the tea upon the warmer.

Billy, our page, appeared a moment later and handed Holmes the lady in questions card.

"Lady Matilde Phillimore," he read aloud before handing it to me.

"Show her up Billy."

Holmes' moods could be unpredictable as well as mercurial and one never knew if he'd fail to rise from his chair for a Baronet or would put on a great show of making a char woman feel welcomed.

Today he greeted Lady Matilde Phillimore with every courtesy, seeing her comfortably seated and supplied with tea and a biscuit.

"I would not have intruded upon you," she said in voice like silk, "had it not been for the counsel of my dear friends, Mrs. Henry Fyldene and Lady Brampton, both of whom have been helped by you Mr. Holmes."

I knew of Mrs. Fyldene as we had been of service in the strange case of the disappearance of Henry Fyldene, her son, but I had no recollection of ever hearing the name of Lady Brampton.

When our guest lifted her black veil I was taken immediately by her beauty and the openness in her sincere sky-blue eyes.

"You may already have heard Gentlemen, that

my husband, Justice Sir Thomas Phillimore, has been missing, two days and two nights thus far now. And before you tell me to go to the police Mr. Holmes, trust that I have already done so. They have put two seasoned Inspectors upon the case and assure me that answers will be forthcoming."

"But that isn't enough for you, your ladyship."

"It certainly is not Mr. Holmes and you may rest assured that money is not a concern in this case. I've been reminded lately of how cheap words can be so allow me to place a firm solidness to my statement. Should you deliver my husband to me alive within the next 72 hours I shall hand you a check worth £20,000 pounds sterling Mr. Holmes."

The lady was perhaps in her mid-thirties and her forthright manner marked her out as a rare soul, but her words had commanded all our attention. I could see that even Holmes, who was the most unaffected man when it came to money, respected her ladyship's willingness to put such a figure to her desires.

"My husband is a most honorable man and even before our marriage I was struck by his personal standards and conduct. I need not tell you, working in your field of criminal detection, how rare such a man is and as his wife I will do all I can to aid in his return."

"You are a Milne are you not your ladyship?"

"That's correct, from Roxburgh in Scotland, but

pray how did you know that."

"I must confess it was your ring, the Moline Cross, the crest of the Milne's."

"Quite true, what the French refer to as the Croix Ancrée, the anchor cross," she smiled.

Holmes' mention of the Milnes brought a news item to mind, one from the time of their betrothal. It had somewhat insensitively called the marriage a joining together of family fortunes or bank accounts as I recall.

"I assure you Mr. Holmes, I am from solid stock and am in no way prone to histrionics. So I ask you to speak plainly and tell me if you believe there is any chance that my husband is still alive."

"The Justice is well known your ladyship and not merely by the upper strata's either," Holmes said, stressing this point, "where the name of Sir Thomas Phillimore commands widespread respect. He is also widely known among the poorest of London's inhabitants and especially so among the criminal elements."

"That is true Sir and my husband has mentioned the fact more than once, that a man in his position makes enemies in all quarters."

Holmes' eyes flashed at these words but he was quick to go on.

"He did well to warn you," he smiled, "but, as you've asked me to speak plainly your ladyship, it my view is that he still lives and may, all things considered, be returned to you in time for breakfast."

While Lady Matilde Phillimore had declared herself not inclined to histrionics these few words of Holmes, delivered so suddenly and so emphatically as they were, undid her utterly. She swooned upon the settee and would have come off completely had not my friend had the wits to catch her.

Holmes had always had a deep affinity for the dramatic and he had shocked me upon countless occasions. Others, however, were not always up to his little peculiarities.

"I'm afraid I've delivered you another patient Watson," said he, with a guilty frown.

"She has lost her husband," I snapped severely, "and despite her best brave face she had to have assumed him dead. Then you launched into that, what was that? A fairytale? For in her wildest imaginings she could not have seen her husband joining her in time for breakfast."

I couldn't imagine what had gotten into my friend but I had a patient to see to and he returned silently to his chair. My scolding may have seemed harsh to him but I believed it a timely reminder that he should exercise greater care in cases where great tension existed.

It took nearly ten minutes and more than one application of smelling salts to bring her ladyship back to herself. Even then I feared a sudden relapse as I had noted often in my past experience and I remained seated next to her, prepared to act if I must.

"Gently now," I said quietly to Holmes, but my eyes communicated my true meaning. "She is in a delicate state just now."

"I'm very sorry," she stuttered out, "I should not have allowed myself to be...overcome, but nothing could have prepared me for...your words Sir."

"It was all me your ladyship and Dr. Watson has given me a good talking to. I should have moderated my words."

"But did you truly mean what you said Mr. Holmes, for I could forgive you all if you would just tell me it was not all a cruel joke at a lady's expense."

Now it was my friend's turn to be stunned for whatever Sherlock Holmes might be, he was not a callous brute.

"I assure you that my words were most sincere and without wishing you further suffering, I hope to deliver your husband safe to your arms in the near future."

"Oh Mr. Holmes, you have given me hope and even if it should last only a day or two, it has saved me. Mrs. Fyldene knew her son dead and gone, a hundred times over, and by weeks' end she said, you marched the young man into her morning room cap in hand. I pray that you may, by all the gifts granted you by Almighty God, repeat that miracle with my own sweet Thomas."

"But if you feel able your ladyship," he said in his kindest voice, "could you answer one question for me.

"I feel quite myself again," she replied, "thanks to your kind ministrations Dr. Watson. Thank you so much."

"Do you remember if your husband made any statements about the murder case of a poisoner taken in..."

"The Fitzhugh Pomeroy Poisoning Trial!" her ladyship exclaimed. "Poor Thomas said it was the worst case of his career, a nightmare from start to finish. He lamented almost daily Mr. Holmes, for he personally believed that the man to be guilty, but between the barrister and the police the man went free. The key questions were not brought out by the barrister and critical evidence held by the police was lost. Worst of all for a wife, the way the press managed matters it was Thomas who came out being blamed. It was all quite ugly and unfair for him, even if Providence saw to the guilty man in the end."

Her ladyship's reference to the St. Marys Church Murder was not lost on us but the sadness written upon her beautiful face showed how deeply she felt for her husband's reputation.

"If I don't see you in the morning," Holmes offered with a kindly smile, "rest assured I will communicate any advance with you by telegram. In the meantime you must not go out unaccompanied and I will even ask Dr. Watson to be so good as to return with you in the cab and see you to your door."

"Of course," I said, "if I may be of service."

"Do you really think I may be in danger?"

"As your husband was in danger I must form my plans upon the premise that you are also. If I am wrong no one is harmed and if I am correct, you will at least remain safe."

I gathered my hat, coat, and cane and joined Lady Phillimore in the cab. Our journey was made in silence as her ladyship clearly wanted to keep her mind free to think upon all that Holmes had said. I too had been puzzled by so much in my friend's behavior and looked forward to hearing his full explanations.

When we arrived at her door she squeezed my hand gently and thanked me, then she stepped out without a further word and vanished inside. Despite her brave words I could sense her fear.

When I returned Holmes was already gone. He'd apparently wasted no time after we left to clear out completely and all I found was a note upon the table.

"Watson, my apologies for the mystery but after you've put these clothes on take a cab to the north side of Whitechapel High Street and the east side of Osborn. There you will find an unlikely fellow selling matches. Purchase a bundle but lay a five-pound note in his tray, then follow him. He goes by the moniker of Lord Nelson. He is one of my people and may be trusted. He will bring you to me by a variety of back alleys and paths but you will be safe enough with him. SH."

The ragtag collection Holmes had prepared for me included shoes, pants with threadbare knees, a suitcoat and vest of questionable origins, a gray overcoat that had once been black, a floppy cap called an Irish Tourer, and even a burlap sack filled with what looked like a half-dozen potatoes. Then I saw the post-script he'd left me.

"1. Very sorry about the fragrance. 2. The bag of stones makes and excellent weapon. 3. Put one of the charcoals from the grate and put it in your pocket. After you've gotten your cab rub it on you whiskers to give you the proper look. Don't do it before you get your cab or you'll have no luck getting one. Take it from me. SH."

After my robing I looked in the mirror and shook my head. Even without the coal I had serious doubts that any London cabby would stop for me.

I was wrong and forty minutes later, with darkness falling across Whitechapel, I was dropped at the very corner Holmes had described. I placed the five-pound note in Lord Nelson's match tray and after giving me a good looking over the little man shrugged and led me off to the north. Within minutes in the Whitechapel maze of alleys, bars, tenements, and the like around Flower & Dean Street I was so turned around as to no longer even know which direction was north. At one point the little man stopped and, giving a strange giggle, he leaned in toward me. The scent of anchovies hit me like cricket bat and I drew away involuntarily, even as he spoke.

"T'is 'Ope Lane," said he, grinning widely, "an' ye better 'ope we make it to t'other end!"

I tightened my grip upon the burlap bag and followed him more closely through what was little more than a dark, crowded alley and when we got through I gave a sigh of relief. While a part of me believed the man had been joking with me, the reputation of this part of Whitechapel meant that I would never have gone there of my own accord. A few minutes later in an equally dark and crowded alley he stopped for good.

"Yer on the back of Casson Street 'ere Mis'ter. Chicksand be that'a way," said he pointing north, "an' Finch is whot we jess come in on."

Then he pointed to a two-story wooden hovel so badly dilapidated that it seemed almost comical to think that anyone really lived there.

"Yer up them steps there. Ee's a waitin' for ye."

I looked up the narrow stairway and wondered if it would really hold my weight and when I looked back Lord Nelson had gone and a dozen wild looking folk were eyeing me over. As disreputable as I looked on Baker Street, upon the alley behind Casson Street I looked like a swell fresh for the picking.

"Ah there you are Watson," Holmes muttered as I entered. "I wondered where you'd gotten too."

"T'is 'Ope Lane," I said in as close an imitation of little Lord Nelson as I could muster, "an' ye better 'ope we make it to t'other end!"

Holmes couldn't help but laugh at my words.

"Yes," said he guiltily, "he will have his little laugh after all."

"Indeed," I growled, dropping the bag of rocks upon the sagging wooden floor and joining Holmes

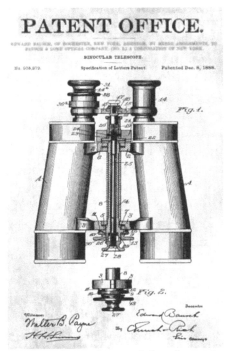

upon the only other piece of furniture in the little room, a rickety chair.

"Well," he said, rubbing his hands together eagerly, "the game is a'foot Watson and I've been planning our campaign."

"Wait just a minute Holmes," I insisted, "what was all that talk back at Baker Street, about getting Lady Phillimore her husband before breakfast?"

"Oh that!" said he, and then he leaned forward suddenly and pointed at a carriage making its way slowly down Casson Street
from the north.

"Here," he snapped, handing me his newest gadget, a brand-new pair of brass Edward Bausch™ binoculars, "tell me what you see."

I put them quickly to my eyes but even through the open window, by the time I'd gotten them focused and with the darkness, there was little I could make out.

"Well, what did you see?"

"I saw nothing," I said, without elaborating.

"That is what I saw as well," he admitted in a statement of defeat, "but that is the second time that carriage has come round in less than an hour Watson and I very much believe he is our man. I am going down into the street. I'll stand just opposite near the door of the tavern. You remain here and I will return after the next round."

"But Holmes, how do you know there will be another round?"

"Because there was a second Watson, so it holds there will be a third."

"Perhaps he has seen all he needed to see."

"Have you never noticed the detailed mind," said he. "It must do things once or in threes. Seldom is it satisfied with twice and rarely does it require a fourth repetition, but one or three, always. As this carriage has passed by twice now, if it is our man, it holds there will be a third time. Then, much later, when the streets are nearly empty and this fog has thickened, he will be ready for the deed Watson."

Holmes, in the disguise of a raucous lout, left as I had come, ordering me to bar it behind him. A minute later I saw him below, crossing the street.

After purchasing a ginger beer inside the packed little place he joined the people outside and found a place to lean his back.

My friend's confidence never ceased to amaze me and as to his mind, what could be made of his theory of one-and-three but rarely two-or-four? Had he written a monograph upon that subject? And as to his monographs, most of which he wrote and sent off to recognized specialists in the field, magazines focused upon the topic, or amateurs who might themselves have explored the topic in their own right, I was probably aware of only a small fraction.

I'd often thought that an entire book made up of a collection of all of Sherlock Holmes monographs, a compendium volume as it were, would be most gladly welcomed by the readers of our adventures.

I had yet to present the idea to Holmes but I'd found him strangely reticent about other such subjects in the past. He had initially baulked at my recording our cases with a mind to publication but had finally given way to my sheer determination. I was affronted by the manner in which the credit for his incredible results went to others without so much as a sidenote. Still, none could call him an encourager of my labors, at least, that is, except in "The Case of the Constant Correspondent" itself, which he had so long pressed for publication.

Chapter 8 - A Game of Wits

We waited an hour, then two, then a third, and my friend's one-and-three theory began to look less impressive with each passing minute. The street had emptied by half as the evening chill, the dangers of the night, and weariness after a long day all called to the residents of Whitechapel and I could tell that even Holmes had begun to wonder.

Then, again out of the north, the same carriage

and pair rounded the corner from Heneage Street and slowly passed down Casson for its third time.

My eyes strained to take note of anything that might be important and this time I saw a lone figure in the rear seat but no one else inside the carriage.

After it had disappeared into the thickening fog toward Whitechapel High Street I looked back at Holmes but he too had vanished. A moment later came a knock and his voice.

"Watson, it is I, do not be afraid," said he, quoting the Bible in everyday conversation as only Sherlock Holmes could do.[20]

"You saw that, did you not?" said he, entering and rubbing his arms for the cold.

"Someone in the rear seat?" I asked.

"Indeed, that means..." he said, letting his words fade.

"That means I now have the time to answer my longsuffering friend's earlier question regarding the getting of Lady Matilde Phillimore's husband, Sir Thomas, before breakfast?"

"Oh that," I said, repeating the very words he had used hours before when the carriage appeared upon its second passage down Casson Street. I remained truly curious about what he had done for it sounded like some sort of fairytale he'd entered into for the beautiful noblewoman. In the regular course the Holmes I knew would have made his excuses, saying that he was in the middle of a critical case and one upon which the very life of his friend,

---

[20] The Gospel of John 6:20.

Dr. John Watson, M.D., depended. He had not done that and instead, in the very middle of the case of the Constant Correspondent, he had entered into the wildest phantasies and promises imaginable.

"At first I was only inclined to be polite Watson, for the woman was most distressed and had mentioned Mrs. Fyldene and Lady Brampton."

"Yes, but who is this Lady Brampton, for I recall Mrs. Fyldene."

"We knew Lady Brampton when she was just an auburn-haired factory girl Watson, do you recall it now?"

"Of course, the peculiar case of the Drummore Treasure, and now she is Lady Brampton? Well, who can say."

"As I said," he continued, "I was only inclined to listen politely, but then something strange happened which, by your reaction, I take it you were not aware."

"I don't know what you refer to," said I, "so I guess we must agree that I was not aware of anything strange in her ladyship's narrative. Then, of course, you launched into that wild fairytale, for so I took it, of her husband joining her for breakfast."

The first point I would draw your attention to was her recollection of her husband's words, 'that a man in his position makes enemies in all quarters.' This struck me as almost prescient Watson, for who was it who had been hung from the rafters of St. Marys Church?"

"Fitzhugh Pomeroy," I replied.

"Then I recalled our correspondent's words in

his last letter. 'You and your allies in their uniforms, their fine robes, their scapulars, and ermines, merely trade upon the suffering of the people.' Could it really be, I wondered, for our killer had dispatched the poisoner, Fitzhugh Pomeroy, because he believed the man had escaped justice. Then her ladyship not only confirmed that it was her husband who presided over the case but reminded us that the way the press handled things, it was Sir Thomas who garnered the lion's share of the blame, while the barrister and the police were all but forgotten."

"Yes, I understand all this, but what has it to do with us Holmes."

"You once pointed out that anyone who could accuse Inspector Caldecott of being a mindless drone, blindly following the directives of the Yard, was a man 'utterly out of touch with reality,' I believe were your exact words."

"Yes, it just showed his ignorance of the realities at the Yard."

"In the same way you referred to his mention of the fine schools I attended without realizing that private tutors had overseen most of my education."

"I also said he had no idea how many dozens of devils you'd put behind bars who curse the name of Sherlock Holmes to this day."

"The principle at play here is that no realist could view Inspector Caldecott and me in the various ways our correspondent did. The man with his feet firmly planted upon terra firma could never say that we were protecting criminality. It is an untenable position; would you not agree?"

"Completely," I said, still lost for the point my friend was obviously driving at.

"So you wouldn't be surprised if the man who has so misjudged us had also done the same with Justice Sir Thomas Phillimore, my supposed 'ally in robes and ermines' and the man the press blamed for the failure to convict Fitzhugh Pomeroy?"

"Holmes," I barely whispered, comprehending the awful truth for the first time, "are you saying that our killer...has Sir Thomas?"

"That's exactly what I'm saying Watson. It only holds that the man who would set the record straight by killing Fitzhugh Pomeroy would ultimately get around to punishing the man who set Pomeroy free."

"But you and I both know, Holmes, that that's not what happened."

"We know, but how did you put it? 'This man comes up with the most trumped-up rubbish.' His knowledge of the Pomeroy Poisoning Trial likely comes from the papers which blamed Sir Thomas Phillimore for the miscarriage of justice. So we cannot expect his judgment to be any more correct concerning Sir Thomas than it was of Inspector Caldecott or me."

"And he did refer to the robes and ermines and to prospering off the suffering of the people."

"As I see it, if we fail tonight, Justice Sir Thomas Phillimore will die on Casson Street in Whitechapel Watson."

"This is all incredible," I muttered.

"We are the man's last hope," Holmes replied, "so here is the plan. The north end of Casson is the least populated and busy, if we can say that of an area packed with people. Comparitively, however, there is a marked difference and our man will have noted that."

"But why Casson Street?"

"It was his plan all along and I believe he had all seven victims chosen and the details of their deaths and displays determined before the first one died. He discovered he had to make adjustments after the crucifixion of Gam Tzomides and he put these into play only after Big Pat Langford resisted him. Always though, he has killed them in the locations he noted on his first, coded letter, only after his adjustments the location of their displays was changed to more frequented, high-visibility areas. However Watson, I believe there was something in our man that thought of killing one of England's most revered judges in a place like Casson Street, in what the people themselves call, "the Wyldes of

Whitechapel,' as a very fitting fulfillment of justice."

"I see, so he will kill Sir Thomas here and no doubt put him up, as he has most of the others, in places he hopes will get the most attention."

"Just so, and as there is a small slaughter house and yard on the north end of Casson, I suspect that is the place our killer will choose to carry out his dark deed."

"But surely Holmes, ther will be someone there, if for no other reason than to keep thieves out."

"No doubt my good fellow, but even five pounds would be a fortune to the night man, would it not? And all he has to do is leave his post for a half hour and wash the spot down afterward."

"When you put it that way," I said, "it strikes me that this killer has no more conscience than did Bram Stibbe, the killer."

"In his mind Watson, he is the solution to the problem of injustice. However, as we can see with Justice Phillimore, our killer has the wrong man. In a world where every man took the right of judge, jury, and executioner upon themselves, how often would their decisions be wrong? In the end, how much evil would be done and how quickly the whole world would spin out of control. No, the system we have, the judge and jury of twelve select-men, requires constant vigilance and improvement, but it is a far better solution than a world of chaos and murder. So the execution of the judge he blames for freeing the poisoner, Fitzhugh Pomeroy, in a slaughter house on Casson Street of all places, just one street away from Flower & Dean Street and in the heart of the Wyldes, is the perfect justice."

"So that's where it will be done?"

"You will be a few doors south, in the shadows, and I will be a few doors to the north. When they open the doors to our killer, we strike Watson. If I'm wrong about this, and the carriage continues on, I will leave my post and follow directly behind the carriage and you will proceed unhurriedly upon the walk. A lone man moving slowly will alarm no one and I will be invisible in my place. Regardless of where the carriage stops, we must strike while they are still upon the street and before our killer has a chance to react. Kill our killer if you must Watson, but protect yourself and Sir Thomas at all costs."

I'd seen Holmes upon the hunt before but this time he was like a coiled spring pressed down. Whatever was to happen tonight I felt it would be momentous, for good or bad, but I had been given my orders, protect myself and Sir Thomas at all costs.

My friend had a theory that a good percentage of the evil done at night occurred in the two hours between one and three. Yet, as of two-thirty all we'd seen moving down Casson Street was the fog. Holmes was in his position not a block north of me and would hear and see the carriage first, if indeed he was correct about its return. I was tucked in behind a staircase and in its shadow I could watch much of the street without being seen. At 2:40 by my pocket watch I heard the first, faint clip-clops of horses hooves and stepped forward to see the same carriage now veering sharply toward the curb in front of the exact place Holmes had predicted, the slaughter house and yard.

Even as two men stepped down onto the curb my feet would not move. Then I saw that the second man moved as if he were drugged and enfeebled by whatever experience he had endured and that settled matters for me. I sprang out and in a dozen steps I was leaping upon the pair like an apparition out of the mist. There were screams and we crashed to the walkway, rolling and wrestling. A bright light from the interior of the slaughterhouse fell upon us but it only revealed the back of the culprit as he sprinted in and vanished from sight. Holmes was on the spot in a second and screamed when he saw that the villain had already fled. Then he too sped into the building.

I rose stiffly and pulled the man up. He was barely conscious and clearly heavily sedated. I put him back into the carriage and ordered the driver to take us back to Baker Street. He seemed unsure what to do when I flashed my revolver he was decided.

Holmes had told me that if I were fortunate enough to get Sir Thomas alive I was to get him to safety and he would join the two of us later. I didn't believe he imagined I'd possibly be able to commandeer the same carriage though. When we finally reached 221B I demanded the driver step up with me and he reluctantly set the brake and helped me with Sir Thomas Phillimore, for so I took the man I'd rescued.

"What is your connection to this business?" I

demanded even as I gave warm tea to my patient.

"I 'ave no connection to any business," the man insisted, "that is, I were hired for the night, to drive these two gents about Whitechapel and drop them where ye found us, then to take them up again and deliver them to a final address they would supply me. They paid a pretty penny too to get me into the Wyldes too, I can tell ye."

"Who hired you?"

"A young chap, 'andsome 'ee were, in a French sort'a way."

"What do you mean?"

"You know guvnor," said he, gesturing about his face with his hand. "'Ee 'ad a showy moustache and one of those things upon 'is chin, you know, the kind'a pointed beard."

"A goatee?" I asked.

"Aye guvnor, that's just the thing, and 'ee were short and light with quick, dark eyes, like most a' those fella's 'ave, ye know?"

"And what was his address?"

"'Ee hired me from my own stall 'ee did and paid well, never gave me an address though, except to pick 'em up at St. Mary's Church and set 'em down 'ere at 2:45 an' wait for 'em."

I asked the man several more questions but it was soon obvious that he was what he seemed to be. I took his name, address, and carriage number from his license and let him go his way. The whole thing had taken less than ten minutes and the man was away. Holmes could always seek the man out if he wanted to ask more questions.

I turned to ladling the hot soup which Mrs. Hudson had prepared and put upon the warmer for the specific purpose, into my patient and slowly he began to rouse himself. Finally near on five in the morning he looked up at me and said, "Who are you?"

"I am Dr. John Watson and you are?" I asked.

"I'm Thomas Phillimore," the man said groggily, then he shook his head and began again, "that is to say I am Justice Sir Thomas Phillimore." Then he tried to raise himself and even drugged I had a hard time holding him down.

"I must see my wife and let her know..."

"No doubt you'll breakfast with your wife this very morning your lordship," I said and he slowly relaxed back upon the settee.

"Who are you?" he said again, focusing.

"I am Dr. John Watson."

"The author?" he asked with surprising clarity.

"Just so your lordship," I answered.

"I like your stories Sir, by Jove I do. A gift that, I'd say and I've always been proud to know you were an Englishman."

I didn't argue over my Scottish heritage as I knew that much of what the man was saying was the result of coming out of his drug induced state. I'd seen it before although Sir Thomas' words were more lucid than most. The important thing was to keep them calm during the process and then, at five sharp he declared himself sleepy and turned upon his side and began snoring like a short line locomotive pulling a load. I covered him with a blanket and threw some coal upon the fire. I would have liked nothing better than to stretch out in my own bed and get some sleep myself but I partook of Mrs. Hudson's soup myself and worked to stay vigilant.

I was looking out the window when a cabby appeared out of the fog which still hung upon the city and Holmes jumped down. His hat was missing, his hair was amiss and a bloodied handkerchief bound his right hand. He fumbled with the key as the cabby moved on and finally he came bounding up the stairs and in.

He stood in silence looking from me to the man snoring upon the settee and simply said, "Safe?"

I nodded and yawned.

"I see you had an eventful morning," I said, motioning him to the table.

"He escaped me Watson, that's the sum of it all. But he gave me a devil of a time before he finally shook me for good...and he knows Whitechapel better than even me. Not a small thing that. And..."

Holmes' words had rushed out of him at high speed and I could tell the fire was still running through his veins.

I held my hand up and pointed to his hand.

"Yes, that, I'm afraid I was a bit cavalier. Grabbed the top of a wall and found it had glass embedded all along it."

"I need to see to this Holmes," I said, "and for that you will have to be absolutely still."

"I see," he said, his sharp eyes darting left and right with nervous energy. "Go on Doctor, do what you must. I will remain still. You may count on it."

I brought my bag and some medicines out and was about to begin when a sleepy voice from the settee called out.

"Who are you?"

"I am Sherlock Holmes your lordship."

"I say," said he nobleman, clearly impressed. "I recently met your biographer somewhere."

"Right here would be my guess," Holmes said, motioning in my direction.

I had my back to our guest and turned and wished him a good morning.

"I say, was it you chaps who got me out of that tight spot?"

"It was indeed Sir Thomas and at your wife's behest."

"I don't know but that there was something wrong with that devil Mr. Holmes."

At this revelation, which fitted well with my own views of our correspondent, I stared pointedly at Holmes. He, as was his way, completely ignored me.

"He talked so much rot I could scarcely stomach his company and I told him so," Sir Thomas continued, still emerging from the effects of the drug he'd been given.

He and Holmes continued to talk for the next hour as I cleaned, mended, stitched, and bandaged a good half dozen cuts in my friend's hand.

"Thank you Watson. I feel as good as new," he said, shaking his hand and grimacing at the shooting pain.

"Maybe not quite good as new," I replied.

At 8 o'clock we walked in on Lady Matilde Phillimore and the shock of the event, thankfully joyous, was greater even than I expected.

When Holmes had declared what I had called his "fairytale," I'd been full of questions and doubts, but here we were. I couldn't argue with my friend's results even when his methods of achieving them mystified me. His ability to make sense out of the seemingly incomprehensible always took me by surprise.

As we left the happy couple and hailed a cab the fog over London was beginning to lift and it looked like a bright day awaited us.

"Will you see to this Watson," said he as he handed over Lady Phillimore's check for twenty-thousand pounds, "and put it in all the right places."

I'd become Holmes accountant and business partner almost by default and as the result of his own pressing desire to have nothing to do with what he saw as an onerous chore. I saw the extraordinary piece of paper safely into my pocketbook and nodded.

"The thing is Watson, and I very much regret it, our correspondent now knows that I solved his puzzle and next time he'll be more than prepared for us."

"We took him by surprise this time though, did we not?"

"Completely my good fellow and the man still bested us."

"How can you say that when we just left Sir Thomas Phillimore alive and well and in the arms of his beautiful wife?"

"Well," said he, acknowledging my point with a moment of silence, "there is that and it was a heated chase."

"Indeed," said I, "and we have this as well!" I added, patting my suit pocket where the check resided.

Holmes had left Justice Sir Thomas Phillimore with instructions to request a police escort whenever he ventured out and at least one to be stationed in his home until "the troubles" were resolved.

"What did you make of the man?" Holmes asked as our Hansom rattled across the cobbles.

"You mean when I confronted him in front of the slaughterhouse?"

"Yes, you took him to the ground did you not?"

"I never did?" I admitted. "He spun out of my grip," said I, "and Sir Thomas, in his weakened condition, and I, tumbled to the pavement."

"So you never once had hold upon him?"

"It was like grabbing at air Holmes," I confessed. "And all I saw was a black cape, otherwise he might have been a spirit for all that. Although how he evaded my grasp when it was all a surprise to him, I cannot say."

"Indeed," Holmes muttered, "and for me as well my good fellow, a black cape and grasping at air."

"He does have you by a good twenty-years or so Holmes," I reasoned, "and a lithe young man of 5 foot 6 or 7 might get many a place you could not."

"Very true," he agreed somewhat to easily.

"What is it?" I insisted. "What's troubling you?"

He shook his head but said nothing.

"What is it?" I demanded again.

"Did he strike you as a lithe young man of 5 foot 6 or 7 might?"

As I paused deep in thought Holmes snapped irritably.

"Think Watson, next to the bulk of Sir Thomas, at a solid 15 stone and 6 feet, did the man seem his inferior for size, or more like his equal."[21]

"He was not dwarfed by Sir Thomas," I said, matter-of-factly. "Though I saw them clearly for only a second his form was not inferior to that of the Justice."

"Excellent," said Holmes. "You see Watson, if the devil is in the details then our impressions of mere moments become our only data. Your view, that the man was not inferior in size to that of the Justice, fits with the impressions I had upon the chase. As much as I would like to hold to the view that I am as much the athlete I was in my mid-twenties, it is a pipe dream Watson but I was not outpaced by our correspondent.[22] On the contrary, the chase went on a good long time, all the way to Merceron Lane, where, with my hand in tatters, I lost him."

"Yes Holmes, but my opinion might easily have

---

[21] Stone: an ancient English unit of measure for body weight which is still in use today throughout the United Kingdom. One stone is equal to 14 lbs. 15 Stones would be 210 lbs.

[22]"Pipe Dream" is an allusion to the dreams brought about by opium. Opiates were widely used by the English literati in the 18th and 19th centuries. Source: phrases.org.uk

been unduly effected by the man's coats and cape? And, in my professional opinion, you remain unusually fit for your age."

"A man's bulk may be changed very easily, as you say, with the addition of the correct articles of clothing, but his height is not nearly so easily manipulated, especially where rapid movement is required. As to my fitness, in a field of mature men no doubt I would shine brightly enough, but against a pack of young men in their twenties, I blush to consider the outcome. You may rest assured that my words are not the fruit of any kind of humility Watson, but of good, old-fashioned honesty."

"Could our man have hired another to serve as a decoy, as it were?"

"Had he known I'd broken his code Watson, then anything might have been possible. However, I can't believe he would provide his adversary with a 'murder map' if he thought for one moment that I might actually decode it. So, no Watson, I don't believe he has brought anyone else in on his secret."

"And as I told you, the carriage driver said he was hired by a handsome young man with a moustache and goatee."

Chapter 9 – The Ramshackle Man

A full week had passed since our first letter from the Constant Correspondent and Holmes had spent two fruitless nights in watching the seventh point identified on what we called "The Murder Map." The first five murders had come in quick succession but after the rescue of Sir Thomas Phillimore our killer had gotten cold feet. Just two letters had followed that event.

The first, which was the sixth letter we had received, had obviously been sent before the planned killing on Casson Street had fallen through. It boasted of the murder of Holmes' "crooked ally" and called Justice Phillimore a "Trading Justice." This term was one used for corrupt justices who made money off of their positions, sending one man down and setting another free based upon who and how much was paid. The letter had come with a broadside from the late 1700's or early 1800's called "The Rat Trap" which condemned the corruption of the bench at that time. Clearly our correspondent wanted us to tie Sir Thomas Phillimore to the "Trading Justices" of that earlier time.

The last letter, the seventh we'd received, was quite different. It was the first letter sent to us after our killer discovered Holmes had broken the code and we'd rescued the Justice.

You gave me the devil's own time of it Mr. Holmes, that you did, but my legs had you by twenty-years at least and as I told you, Whitechapel

is my world, it is not yours. I was born here and there isn't a single square foot I don't personally know. The truth is you never had a chance to take me, but you made a good run of it, Old Man, no doubts. Now, as to my little puzzle, how did you do it? Come on now. Discovering that you had solved it was truly unnerving you know. I talked myself into believing that I'd supplied you with a few additional clews which neither you nor any other man would ever be able to make use of. It was a double clew system, yet the lines were parallel and unconnected, effectively forming two puzzles each dependent upon the other to be solved. Yet, when le bon docteur rushed out of the fog upon me, that was, how do you say, the rude awakening! That was the moment I first knew that Sherlock Holmes was better than I had believed him. So now you know my secrets and you've foiled me at the sixth turn. So what am I to do? Shall I select a new victim to replace Sir Thomas or should I simply move on to the unfortunate man selected as my next victim? As I have played this game fairly from the first I

*suppose I must tell you either way, even as this puts
all the advantage on your side.*

*You would no doubt want me to move on,
making one less body for the morticians, but then
you recall your friend, Dr. John Watson, who
would come to my attention all the sooner should I
ignore a sixth victim. What is the great detective to
do. I will move on Mr. Holmes. The seventh victim
will become the sixth and the doctor will serve as
my new number seven. Oh, and by the way, had you
simply raised your hand parallel to your shoulder in
the dark of Merceron Lane you would have touched
my face. As I said, you gave me the devil's own time
of it Mr. Holmes."*

"It's one thing with these fellows when they think
they can get away a thing," I remarked to Holmes
and Inspector Caldecott, "but it's another when they
know they're playing for keeps."

"Correct Watson, he had it all his way through
the first five murders and that never bothered him.
We had it only with Sir Thomas and he is already
voicing his many complaints."

"Is there anything in the letter you'd bring to my
attention Mr. Holmes?"

"Five items Inspector," Holmes replied that
certain way he had with such things. "The first is the
surprising maturity in his handling of the great
setback upon Casson Street. So complete a failure,
it seems to me, would have been most distressing to
a man in his twenties. Yet our correspondent takes
it all in stride."

"That is odd," I agreed.

"The second point is his comment that he had the advantage of me in the chase in two ways. The first were his legs, 'my legs had you by twenty-years at least.' The other was his intimate knowledge of Whitechapel, "this is my world, it is not yours. I was born here and there isn't a single square foot I don't personally know.'"

"How does this help me Mr. Holmes?"

"Just that with such advantages in those two vital areas he is, later, unconscious of his slip when he says that I gave him 'the devil's own time of it,' and that had I simply raised my hand parallel I would have touched him. Do you see the contradiction involved here Inspector Caldecott, for I assure you that it is too great to be real?"

"I'm afraid that, at the risk of appearing stupid, I do not Mr. Holmes."

"It is simply this Inspector; our killer could not have had both the advantages of younger legs and a more complete knowledge of Whitechapel and not completely lost me in the first two blocks. That he can admit later that I would have taken him in Merceron Lane when I stopped, as I indeed did, had I but raised my hand, disproves the truths of one or both of his former statements."

"That is one of the most incredible displays of detective work I've ever seen Mr. Holmes," the Inspector exclaimed.

Holmes ignored this declaration of honest praise without the slightest pause.

"The third point is the complexity of the double-puzzle itself."

As Holmes paused I asked about his statement, for I could not put it together for the life of me.

"Only that the complexity is itself evidence Watson, and in this case it is evidence of an intelligence of the first order."

"And the fourth Mr. Holmes?"

"It is the statement, 'when le bon docteur rushed out of the fog upon me, that was, how do you say, the rude awakening!' This statement is illustrative on two points. First, the use of 'le bon docteur' is odd. It is simple French and might be used by any number of educated Englishmen, in passing and without the least significance."

"But our man declared himself completely self-educated," I reminded.

"And as such one would not have expected the phrase to pass his lips, as you say Watson. Yet, as it is used by him and in conjunction with the impossible phrase, 'how do you say, the rude awakening,' we cannot fail to take notice."

"How's that? How is it impossible?" Inspector Caldecott asked.

"Look at it again Inspector," Holmes replied with surprising patience. "'how do you say, the rude awakening.' Now you say it as you would, naturally, to us," he commanded.

"Well," the Inspector began, obviously thinking about it. "I suppose I would say something like, 'how do we say it, a rude awakening."

"Exactly, your words declare your membership within the group, that being the English. "How do 'we' say?"

"And our killer wrote, 'how do you say,'"

"Demonstrating his own membership outside the group. 'How do you English say?' and not, 'How do we English say?'"

"And with rude awakening I'd likely say, 'a rude awakening,' but what does that tell us?"

"It shows an ease with the language, Inspector. Some terms are used in formal settings but demonstrate no less comfort operating within a language. The phrase, 'the rude awakening,' shows not a greater formality than, 'a rude awakening,' it shows an awkwardness with the language."

"So in a way," I said, "these two taken together point to our man being a Frenchman?"

"I would say that it is a possibility we must seriously consider Watson. Recall that despite telling us that he was born and raised in Whitechapel and was wholly self-educated on top of that, we have at least some evidence that appears to contradict both those statements. If this were the only irregularity in his correspondence that would lessen its value, however, again we have the earlier evidence that our correspondent is attempting to mislead us. Did he not say that he had both the advantage of youth and familiarity over me and yet failed to outdistance me."

"If you had raised your hand...you would have touched my face," the Inspector repeated.

"Exactly, that is how I see these as well."

"The one statement contradicting the other," I clarified.

"Quite so Watson. It is completely possible that our killer is an athletic young man, twenty-odd years my junior and born and raised in Whitechapel. I do not dispute that. What is impossible however, and what I do dispute, is that such a man would not have lost me utterly over such a distance."

"So, if I'm on the same page now Mr. Holmes, it is possible for our killer to be born and raised in Whitechapel and to be self-educated, as it were, but not to be that and use phrases like 'le bon docteur' and 'how do you say, the rude awakening?'"

"You have grasped it fully Inspector Caldecott. "You see, the great challenge to inhabiting another character, if that is indeed what our Constant Correspondent is attempting to do, is to keep from lapsing into one's true self."

"And is great intelligence alone the antidote to that failing Holmes?" I asked, for I'd learned that my friend was not only a genius at identifying the shortcomings in a crime, but also at knowing how they might have been allayed or eliminated entirely.

"It is not Watson, although it is a benefit. I have found that the only remedy to this particular challenge is practice. The actor practices his lines again and again but it is the veteran actor who has mastered not only the memorization but the delivery as well. Clearly our killer has planned his crimes extensively and, no doubt, over years. He even envisioned his interaction with me and saw that as an even greater challenge, but the practice..."

"Was lacking," Inspector Caldecott nodded.

"And the final point Holmes?"

"It is in his statement Watson, 'That was the moment I first knew that Sherlock Holmes was better than I had believed him.' We've already seen this man's brilliance, his genius even in certain aspects of his work, evil as it is, but this statement reveals a weakness in our man."

The Inspector looked on in obvious confusion but couldn't bring himself to admit again that he had failed to grasp Holmes' point. Having been in the same place many times myself I felt for him.

"I've heard you say many times Holmes that the fool underestimates his enemy or his challenge, while the wise man seeks a realistic estimation or even errs on the side of overestimating his opponent by a few degrees at least."

"Underestimating me demonstrates that while this man has taken naturally to killing and is skilled at planning murder, even at posing and arranging his subjects, he remains the amateur when it comes to appraising his opponent. He lacks the experience of the practiced criminal or tactician and, in this case, he doesn't even realize what he is giving away in his statement. You see inspector, underestimating an opponent is an extremely dangerous practice. I have even gone so far as to call it the fatal flaw of a criminal. Sooner or later, for the man who exhibits this trait, will trip himself up."

"He'll give the game away," Inspector Caldecott smiled.

"Indeed he will."

"And has our man, our Constant Correspondent done that Holmes? Has he given the game away."

"He has given us much Watson and based upon what I see, it is now only a matter of time on his side and of vigilance upon our own. Although I admit that for you personally, who will soon be the target of this man if we cannot stop him, my words are of little comfort."

"You know Holmes," I reminded, "I told you that the Casson Street carriage driver said the man who hired him was young and handsome 'in a French sort of way.'"

"That is something," Holmes replied vaguely.

"What? You don't credit it?"

"No, I do Watson. I only try to reconcile facts."

"What is there to reconcile?" I demanded. "For the driver had no reason to lie did he for our man had not even expected us that night."

"The man who saw me in Merceron Lane, if he were the man described by the driver, would have outstripped me by a quarter mile in the mile. Are we agreed upon that Watson?"

"I suppose we are," I replied.

"Then who was the man hiding an arm's length from me in Merceron Lane?"

"I see," I admitted. "This is a dark business is it not?"

"It is indeed Dr. Watson and for me, I fear, matters become more...confused."

"I fear it is a deucedly twisted cord we've got hold of Gentlemen," Holmes declared, "and no doubt the result of years of preparation. In our man's sheer determination I see the evidence of a clear and great hardening toward the criminal classes, not that this is hard to believe for many share it no doubt. The speed with which he dispatched Big Pat Langford, for someone who was not a hardened criminal if we are to believe his own admission, is proof of such a tempering. All together it has made for a deep and complex mystery."

"Very like his double-clewed and coded murder map Mr. Holmes."

"Very correct Inspector and as to our plan, Watson is free to stand guard with me again on Fieldgate Street tonight, so I won't require any of your men. If our killer does not strike, then I will move to the ramshackle house at Darling Row and Lisbon Street and watch again for those passing by. And yes Watson, I will be alert for the young, mustached man with a goatee who is handsome 'in a French sort of way.'"

"Have you had any luck on that front Mr. Holmes?"

"I failed to find the young, athletic young man of five feet seven or eight inches, with the smooth-soled dress shoes of a clerk or teller, dark brown mid-length hair, and the bandaged left hand, at least within the period he would have likely worn such a thing. Since receiving the broader description from the carriage driver I've identified four candidates for our Constant Correspondent. I've tracked two to their homes and workplaces and neither fits with the clews."

"So two more chances then?"

"As you know Inspector, our field of endeavor requires endless hard work and a part of that is the presence of countless dead ends. If our killer only knew the secret to my solving his puzzle he wouldn't believe it for a minute."

"Well what was it Holmes? Tell us!" I insisted.

"But I just did Watson, for it was simply the willingness to work at it. I applied 1253 possibilities to the double-clews before everything finally fitted together, and mathematically speaking I might easily have had to do far more than that."

"I have to say Mr. Holmes, that the more I get to know you, the more amazing you are to me. You spoke of the determination of our killer but Sir, I'd say you've surpassed even him."

After the Inspector's departure Holmes sat down with his map again and showed me Fieldgate Street.

"Fieldgate is a problem Watson and I'll show you why. In its short two blocks it has at least seven lanes opening on its southern side," he pointed out. "Plumbers Street, Valford, Greenfield, Settles Street, Nottingham Place, Myrdle Street and Romford. Meanwhile, to the north is the yard of St. Marys Church, where our man hung the infamous poisoner out for show. It has a high stone fence along the western half of its length and an even higher cast iron fence running the remainder of the length of Fieldgate Street."

"And what is this?" I asked, pointing to a short lane running into the church yard.

"That is a delivery lane, gated and locked except for the few occasions when it is in use."

"So how many doors actually open upon Fieldgate itself?"

"That is our problem Watson, you've spied it straight away. There are four residential doors between Plumbers and Valford at the western end. Another six doors to tenements between Greenfield and Settles Street nearer the center of the street's length and just two on the eastern end between

Romford Street and New Road, which marks the end of Fieldgate."

"Just twelve doors in what, a block and a half?"

"And that's the trouble with Fieldgate. A man could easily watch the entire thing if he were not devilishly exposed in front of the stone fence opposite."

"On a clear night perhaps," I forwarded.

"Yes and we have two men, but how to do it, for I tell you he will be on the alert this time. I wonder what could have induced him to choose Fieldgate."

"Surely Holmes, it is as you said, the man never dreamed you could actually solve his code."

"Very true, so Fieldgate was selected without regard to observation."

"There is also your theory that our killer would likely select places for his crimes where he was most comfortable. So if, as you believe, the ramshackle upon Darling Row and Lisbon Street was his place of birth and is now not far from his personal residence, then..."

"You've done it again Watson."

"Done what Holmes?"

"You've cast the light upon our man's reasoning. Fieldgate, my dear fellow, was chosen precisely for its nearness to this man's workplace. You are a great conductor of light," Holmes remarked sincerely. "I am most indebted to you. I will immediately leave Watson, in disguise, and walk that area to see which businesses may be along there or abut upon Whitechapel High Street."

"There is no need Holmes," I replied happily, "for you will recall I made a survey of the businesses in that area which might provide employment to a clerk or teller and here is my list."

I rose and went to my pocket notebook and removed four sheets of handwritten notes and handed them to my friend.

"This is capital Watson," said he with his gleeful expression of earnest delight. "Capital!"

He spent the next hour bent over the map and my notes, placing pins, assigning street numbers and otherwise muttering to himself nonstop. One of the first "truths" which Holmes had shared with me was how great a mistake it was to begin theorizing in a case before one had sufficient data. His point being that those who do so, no matter how disciplined their mind, invariably begin to put the facts to a theory, rather than the other way around. According to him only the fitting of theories to facts solves a case.

I had now supplied my friend with four pages of the most detailed notes, double-sided, of the exact area he most desired to study. The data covered the area from the head of Whitechapel High Street where it joined Commercial Street, eastward to St. Mary's Church and included the side streets of Church Lane, Alder Street, and the joint exit at Plumbers & Fieldgate Streets.

I don't know how long it was before I realized he was no longer mumbling to himself and looked up from my desk, but I found him staring at me in sober silence.

"What is it?" I asked, concerned by his manner.

"This bookstore," said he gravely, "what more can you tell me about it?"

"What? Do you mean Chartier & Company?"

"I do," said he, still the soul of sobriety.

"I asked for a book on Forsyth's First Yarkand Natural History Expedition. You may remember, it went into Eastern Turkestan in 1870, but the proprietor was unsure of the subject."

"Can you describe this man?" Holmes asked.

"I recall he was a handsome man with a regal bearing and a most dashing beard, something along the line of Prince Albert, although nearly black in color," I said, pleased to be able to say so much.

"And his age, height, weight, footwear, and name, do you recall any of these things?" Holmes asked, clearly frustrated.

I often operated upon a different page than that of my friend and it had happened once again.

"Of course," I stammered, "a man of perhaps forty and of good height, say six feet even. He is somewhat plump around the middle, perhaps 17 stone.[23] His first name is...Sharle, a name I've never heard before but no doubt an obscure French name, and his surname, fittingly for it matches the bookstore, is Chartier, of which I gather he is very proud."

"And his footwear?"

"I'm afraid..." I offered weakly.

Holmes looked at me disapprovingly.

---

[23] 17 stone at 14 lbs./stone = 238 lbs.

"Watson," said he at last, "the name you put down as being of obscure French origins is, in fact, simply Charles. It is pronounced 'Sharle,' as no doubt Chartier in the French would also have been pronounced 'Shar-tee-yay.' Doubtless the 'Chartier' pronunciation is an accommodation to his English neighbors."

"Well," said I defensively, "I see little import to the pronunciation of the man's name Holmes!"

"Truly Watson?" said he, staring hard.

I knew my friend well enough by this time to know he wanted more from me. Perhaps my answers had not been as detailed as he'd desired and I'd failed to observe the man's footwear, an obvious oversight, but I had no idea at what he was now driving.

"The Constant Correspondent? The Concerned Citizen? Monsieur Charles Chartier?"

I stared dumbfounded and speechless at my friend. He had seen it clearly while I had seen nothing.

"Him?" I exclaimed, finally. "He is our Constant Correspondent?"

"Or someone has gone to a great deal of effort to make us believe it."

"But Holmes," I pleaded, "the man is a hefty 17 stones and not a pound less. I cannot imagine him sprinting the lanes and alleys between Casson Street and Merceron, can you?"

"It does seem unlikely," he mused, "but I believe we are on the right trail now Watson. What say you to another visit to Chartier & Company to check on Forsyth's First Yarkand Expedition?"

"But the proprietor was unfamiliar with the subject," I reminded.

"Yes Watson, but perhaps this time you will get a look at the clerk, whom you could have waited for upon your last visit. I would even go so far as to predict he will be wearing smooth-soled dress shoes."

"The clerk...is the ramshackle man?"

Chapter 10 – The Face of a Killer

"It's just that, won't the killer recognize me?"

"No doubt he will, but you've been there before Watson. The proprietor will recognize you. He may even remember which book you were looking for as some of these fellows are sharp dealers."

"So I am to wait for the clerk this time, if he is not there, and then under the guise of purchasing a volume on the First Yarkand Expedition I am to confirm all our evidence?"

"It is a bold move, I agree, but it has the chance

of telling us a great deal about our nemesis," Holmes replied.

I found myself nervous at the thought of facing the man who'd written that I would be his final victim, if Holmes failed to stop him. My friend continued to coach me.

"Including his footwear Watson, you often overlook that information," said he, emphasizing the point I'd missed before with the proprietor.

I was to come up Whitechapel High Street from Commercial and Holmes would come from the opposite direction, out of the northeast.

"I will be just three or four minutes behind you and in disguise. By the time I reach the window you should be in conversation with the killer. Remember to move yourself parallel with the storefront Watson, so as to not block my view of the man. This will be the first time we are able to see him for ourselves."

"Unless of course he is one of the two remaining men from you've seen from the ramshackle house," I noted.

"Yes, that is true, but as you pointed out, I expect the killer to recognize you. Watch for any sign of nervousness on his part, do you understand?"

I nodded, even though my mind was racing and full of doubts.

"Purchase your volume if they have it and act just as you would if this were any other visit to the book sellers. Then, barring the unexpected, leave casually and without any hurry."

"And should the unexpected occur?" I enquired

with more than a little concern.

Inspector Caldecott's words were still ringing their clarion call warning in my ears. He'd said, "I don't think any truly sane man would dare go after the most dangerous men in London. I know if I were tasked with that job I'd fairly blanch at the mere thought of it. You have to remember that we estimated Bram Stibbe's murder count at close on a hundred men and yet your correspondent hunted him down, nailed his hands to a cross, and crucified him almost like he'd done Gam Tzomides!"

As far as I knew I'd be facing the killer of Bram Stibbe in the very near future.

"After you leave the store continue on your path to the northeast but turn down Fieldgate to our meeting point halfway down in the church's little used rear lane. I will continue down Whitechapel High Street by all appearances, but I will actually turn left at the first corner and go down Alder to Mulberry Lane and another left. This will take me all the way around the building the bookstore is in and I'll be sure to inspect the rear entrance. I'll then go through the narrow path leading off Mulberry and across to Plumbers Street then on to Fieldgate to our hiding place. It will be dark by the time we reach our destination."

"Then what Holmes?"

"Then we'll review our findings and when the hour comes I'll watch the two establishments with four tenements each and you'll take the most distant one between Romford Street and New Road. These are the only options our killer has now," Holmes said so quietly I had difficulty making out his words.

"So you think it will be tonight?"

"I do Watson. Either way we have to be ready for him tonight."

When the hour came I walked steadily up the main street of Whitechapel, that area which had so long been called the cesspool of London, where all the dregs of Britain and the world collected. That teeming, irreverent, busy place was alive even in the fading light of evening. When I came to the windows of Chartiers' I couldn't help but look.

The displays had been set out with an admirable care and attention which seemed suddenly odd amidst the surroundings. Old books, classics, their covers familiar as old friends, met my eyes first. A leatherbound first edition of "A Christmas Carol," by Charles Dickens, was given the place of honor. I remembered that it had been published in 1843 by Chapman & Hall. As I passed by came the newer marvels. A clothbound copy of Stevenson's "The Strange Case of Dr. Jekyll and Mr. Hyde," which I hadn't noticed on my last visit, lay upon a cloth of red velvet.

I turned in and pushed the door to the pleasant "cling-cling" of a little bell and Charles Chartier looked up from his desk.

"Ah, how wonderful, you have returned for that book upon, don't tell me, Forsyth's First Yarkand Expedition."

Although I had been as tense as I had been in years the man's manner put me at my ease almost in an instant.

"I'm afraid I forget the year, Sir," he continued apologetically.

"1870," I said, smiling. "You've an impressive memory."

"Oh, thank you, it is a great benefit in the book trade you know."

"I can only imagine, although I have a love of books myself."

"I could tell the instant you walked in upon your last visit he said. Bibliophiles always look upon the books reverentially," said he, "and linger."

With that he called across the room to an unseen person somewhere in the rows of shelves.

"Phillip, you have a lover of books here."

So our killer was named Phillip, I thought, and my body stiffened involuntarily at the thought that I would soon be looking the Constant Correspondent in the eyes.

"Phillip is my specialist upon history, the natural sciences, Egyptology and the Orient," the heavy-set but regal proprietor said suavely, as if he were selling the clerk to me as much as his books. "And would you believe, he is largely self-taught?"

At these last words a chill ran up my spine. I had faced many dangers over the years with Holmes but as I stood in Chartier & Company's bookstore I realized that I usually had my friend at my side.

Then the young man appeared, hunched over and lumbering along awkwardly like the character of the hunchbacked man in Victor Hugo's novel.[24]

---

[24] The Hunchback of Notre-Dame, by Victor Hugo, pub. 1831.

He carried an armload of books which he sat gently down upon his paper-strewn desk.

"Good evening Sir," he said, straightening his back and raising himself up to five feet seven or eight inches. He had dark hair and dark eyes but pale skin which gave him a dramatic air. He was thin with very narrow shoulders and delicate hands. I noticed that his right index finger was black with ink, from which I deduced that he was right-handed. As I looked at the young man's smooth-soled dress shoes I thought of Holmes. No doubt he would be pleased that I noticed.

"Phillip, this is the gentleman I told you about, the one who so interested you. He has come in again about Forsyth's 1870 Yarkand Expedition."

"Yes, to Yakub Beg, the Amir of Kashgar in Turkestan," said the young man knowledgeably and I found myself being suddenly disarmed.

I had expected something very different indeed and the young clerk soon seated me at a large oak table where two large volumes lay closed upon another velvet cloth.

"After Monsieur Chartier told me about your interest I gathered our two, current volumes and prepared them for your inspection," he said in the friendliest manner. His eyes neither avoided me nor remained upon me too long and his manner was natural and relaxed. "I must warn you," he said suddenly, in barely a whisper, as I took my seat at the table. "This volume is a first edition and is substantially more expensive than the other one, but I assure you that both are in excellent condition.

The prices are upon the tabs in the cover and if you have no questions I will leave you to your review of the volumes. I will be just here though and you need only call out."

"Thank you," I said sincerely and turned to the first edition copy and gasped when I saw the price. Unlike the sweep of our correspondent's hand, the price was etched in quite a plain hand, even somewhat rough, from which I realized that the proprietor himself was the one who set the prices.

It was then, just as I prepared to open the tan leather cover that my hand froze and a spasm rushed over me. I had been so transported by the two men and the discussion of the book, and then by the beautiful specimens themselves, that I had forgotten all about Holmes. I had no idea if he had seen the young man, Phillip, or how I had been standing. Had I blocked my friend's view? He must have passed on along the street minutes ago now and was likely even passing behind the building as I prepared to look at the treasures before me.

So far from being filled with terror at the approach of a killer, I'd been put utterly at my ease and no more natural response could have been expected than the one I had received.

The young clerk seemed not only not to recognize me as anything other than an interested customer but he also treated me with the respect which a lover of books gives a fellow bibliophile. Either he was the most practiced of villains or he was exactly what he appeared to be. Then the words of his letters came back to me.

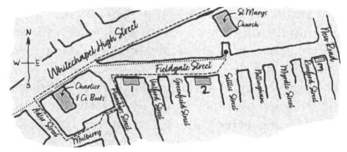

Now, even as my hand hovered over the cover of the first edition, those words flooded my mind.

"I am a man of no importance to anyone except my employer, and he couldn't function without my services."

"My significance...lies in the fact that I will kill."

"I live in Whitechapel and have done all my life. I'll likely die in this place as well and probably mere blocks from the humble ramshackle of my birth, which I pass by almost daily."

"I have no education at all, other than what I have given myself, but I pride myself, as you do, upon my logical mind."

"I will kill seven times Mr. Holmes...and should you fail to stop me in time, there will be an eighth victim, Dr. John Watson!"

It so overcame me that I nearly rose and departed straightaway, which would never have done for Holmes' desire was not to raise any warning flags if it could be helped.

Slowly I returned to my books but the spell that had been cast over me earlier was now irretrievable broken. Even as I appeared engrossed in my full examination of the books my eyes continually crept up to look upon Phillip, who sat not more than fifteen feet away working at his desk. So this was our killer. I now saw him in the light of the threats and insults with which he'd filled those letters and despite the outward appearance of a harmless clerk, which he inhabited perfectly, I knew I was looking upon the killer of Bram Stibbe, the Whitechapel assassin. This was the man who had nailed railroad spikes through the hands of the McAuley Gang's most notorious killer.

It was a chilling revelation and when I rose from the table twenty minutes later, I made sure to force the chair to give a loud skreich against the floor.

"Have you decided upon either of the volumes or would you like us to continue our search?" he asked cordially.

"I will take the less expensive copy," I said smiling as naturally as I could. "As you said, they were both in excellent condition."

"And I know you will be pleased with your purchase, Sir."

After completing the transaction he wished me a "good evening," but even before I'd reached the door the young man had turned his back on me and returned to his work.

"I expected you sooner Watson, is everything alright?" Holmes asked from the shadows where he was virtually invisible. "Here he said, the night will be long and you'll need a heavy coat."

With that he helped me on with my black, wool long coat and pulled me into the shadows. I knew he was all curiosity to hear my report and I told him how the young man had taken me in so completely with his natural behavior."

"But were you not aware at any time that you were in the presence of great danger Watson?"

"I went in expecting to feel that way but I have to admit that only my recollections of his letters could stir me to fear the man."

"Indeed," Holmes muttered as his eyes scanned the dark street still busy with people coming and going.

"What is it?" I asked, for I knew his mind was wrestling with something.

"Consider this my good fellow. If I am correct about what awaits us tonight, this young man was in the middle of contemplating the murder of a sixth victim at the exact time you made your entry to his store and yet you can attest only to his natural and disarming manner."

"It does sound incredible when you put it like that Holmes, but I can only tell you what I know to be so."

"Do you understand my difficulty Watson?" said he almost pleadingly. "That one still so young could have cultivated such skills, such duplicity."

"I do understand and I felt the same thing when I was with the man and yet, when I recalled his letters, I understood. I think he gave us a clue to his true self in that first letter. Do you remember he compared himself to you Holmes? He told us he had no education at all, other than what he'd been able to give himself, but then he wrote that he took pride in his logical mind, 'just as you do Mr.

Holmes.' You have also noted a brilliance in some of his...work. Oh, and Monsieur Chartier let slip that his clerk was largely self-taught and a specialist in the fields of history, natural science, Egyptology and the Orient."

After this we settled into the shadows upon either side of the short alley that ran to a heavy gate and on into the churchyard.

Holmes watched over the tenements between Plumbers and Valford Street at the western end of Fieldgate Street and those between Greenfield and Settles in the center. Meanwhile I kept the smaller building at the eastern end of the street, between Romford Street and New Road, under my watch.

We had begun our vigil early and by eleven o'clock my knees were shaking and my eyes were aching. The people had thinned out but there were still loungers talking, laughing, and roughing about here and there. Holmes had seen nothing of significance other than a few men from various tenements leaving for their night shift duties. I had nothing to report at all. Shortly before midnight we saw a handful of men returning to their rooms and one of them unlocked his door in my section and stepped in. I saw a dim glow as he lit a lamp and then there was a terrible scream and he came running out into the street calling for the police.

Holmes knew it couldn't be a coincidence but to be safe he left me on watch over his end of the street and he ran off to join the growing crowd around Romford Street. Soon I saw him enter and he remained until the police arrived.

He walked back with his hands deep in his pockets and his head upon his chest and I knew something was wrong.

"What is it Holmes?" I asked when he got close.

"We can go Watson. I will tell you all in the cab."

A few minutes later we got a Hansom on Whitechapel High Street and settled in.

"Whatever happened back there," he said, "it was our man."

The weight of his words were obvious. I had failed in my duties. Somehow our killer had gotten in, killed his man, and gotten out with his victim in tow, to put him up where the public would have the best show of it. Try as I might though, I couldn't make sense of it.

"Holmes," I pleaded, "I saw nothing, all night."

He turned his head and even in the darkness I could feel his gaze.

"You misunderstand my meaning Watson," said he wearily. "Whatever happened back there, it happened much earlier in the day. The man who rents that room is a shift worker like so many here. He worked his twelve hours, spent some time at a pub, then came home to sleep. When he lit his lamp it illuminated...a most grisly scene, which I will not try to describe Watson. It is clear that our man had watched this street for some time and knew the habits of the residents here abouts. Apparently it is quite quiet there between nine and eleven in the morning, so much so that someone might have come and gone without being seen."

"This is unbelievable Holmes. Our killer," I said, trying to find the words, "I thought that his killings would all be done at night."

"As did I," said he shaking his head, "but it was only because it had always been so. Nowhere did our man make such a statement or promise. Our assumption left him free to strike at any time and after we had decoded his puzzle he knew he had to change his pattern to a daylight murder. The color of the blood and the consistency of the coagulated matter places the murder to those quiet hours the crowd told me about."

"Between nine and eleven in the morning."

"Just so. He would have seen the workman leave and then simply waited. If he had drugged the victim the way he had Justice Phillimore, they would have been out of a cab in a minute and into the flat."

"But what of a key?" I asked.

"He's had months to work on that Watson, maybe even longer. For all we know he may even have rented that room for a time. When the deed was completed he would have only had to check the street and hail his carriage. Leaving may have taken a little longer but even that would again be mere minutes."

"How?" I cried. "It's one thing to carry a body out in the blackness of night but in the daylight?"

"I have reason to believe that a chest was used in this case. Though the man was in shock over what he'd seen, he confirmed for me that his old sailor's chest was missing.

"Are you saying what I think you are?" I asked with a growing sense of horror. "That this man fit a human body into the sailor's chest?"

"I fear it so, for the room bears testimony to such a deed."

My mind reeled at Holmes words. We'd seen murder and violence before, and danger aplenty, but seldom had we witnessed a case of wanton barbarity to equal just one of the murders which this killer had engaged in.

This said nothing of the staging of the bodies afterward as well. If Holmes were correct and this man had taken his leisure over the course of years, to plan such things, I could hardly agree with my friend upon the point of our killer's sanity.

"Now what?" I enquired, for Holmes sat in

silence and volunteered nothing further.

"We lost our advantage Watson," said he, clearly disturbed by the fact. "This man operated with impunity while we waited for nightfall. Now the last man is dead and we have no idea where the body will be placed."

"But surely, there is no body to display Holmes, at least not as we know it."

"I have no doubt that our Correspondent will go through all the motions he has carried out before."

"But surely, we know who he is now. Let us simply pounce upon him with the Inspector and clap him in irons."

"And hope that a man who has planned every aspect out meticulously will have carelessly left us an abundance of incriminating evidence with which to convict him? No, it will never do Watson. We cannot pounce without the assurance that we can hold our man. Otherwise it will be another failure, as the Fitzhugh Pomeroy trial was, and the Constant Correspondent too will walk free. No, I very much fear that the time has come for Dr. John Watson to disappear."

"Into the American West?" I snapped, in utter disbelief. "Do you really expect me to run away?"

"There is no shame in running my good fellow, as long as it provides us with another day to work against the schemes of our opponent."

I shook my head in the hope of clearing it but nothing helped.

"He'll be coming for you now Watson, unless..."

"Unless what?" I demanded.

"In chess, as sometimes in life, one can upset the opponent's plan with an aggressive offensive which requires the focus to be placed upon defense. It is a gamble Watson and I won't deny it, but as our killer has declared that he won't be taken perhaps some version of your idea has merit."

"We lack hard evidence tying our man to any of the murders."

"Surely the handwriting!"

"Even if he did not cloak his handwriting, as I fully expect he did, would the court convict a man of a capital offense based upon that evidence alone? I think not."

"What then would you suggest?"

"Do you recall his words about allowing us to take him?"

"'I shan't be taken in, Mr. Holmes, nor will I swing for what I've done.' He expected to end his life in Whitechapel as well."

"So, the question for us becomes one of veracity Watson."

"Veracity? I don't see how it plays any part in our considerations."

"I speak of the honesty of our killer. Did he sincerely mean what he said when he said it?"

"I see, will he truly not allow us to take him."

"And will he refuse to run if it comes to that, will he honestly remain even if it means ending it all in Whitechapel."

"Ah, because he said he fully expected to die in Whitechapel."

"Indeed and if we may count upon the man's

veracity, then the simple act of cornering him in an inescapable position will precipitate his end by his own hand."

"Because, as he said, 'I shan't be taken in.'"

"That and his declarations that he wouldn't 'be kept like a base animal in some distant prison' and that I wouldn't do for him as I had 'for so many others. There will be no drum rolls or black flags for the Constant Correspondent, you may put that from your mind altogether.'"

"That is a brilliant gambit Holmes," I declared.

My friend's genius had shown brightly before upon many occasions but faced with the challenge of the Constant Correspondent I saw new things from Holmes. He had called this one of "the most unusual cases of our long career" and justified supporting its publication for "the innumerable instances it afforded to highlight the science of deduction."

Both of these points were undeniably true and yet I had seen deeper into the juxtaposition it held over and against the Ripper Murders, which would come somewhat later. In our case Holmes had played his chess game, as it were, and in conjunction with his brilliant deductions and the uniqueness of the case his, reasoning throughout had so far proven correct.

Instead of giving the killer the full light of the press and allowing the sensationalism of his foul crimes to foment chaos throughout the city, my friend had gone so far as to manipulate evidence, swear officers of the law to silence, and even direct the falsification of official reports. Now, the logic of his "aggressive offensive" was impossible for me to argue.

If our killer had meant what he'd said, then our case had been destined from the beginning never to see the inside of an English courtroom.

"Even if you succeed in running me to earth, I shan't be taken in nor will I swing for what I've done...I am quite resigned to my fate, should it come to that. You will see me play the sportsman as well as any of your class at University. I'll even be so bold as to prophecy my own death. I will die in Whitechapel, mere blocks from the place of my birth, but I shan't be kept like a base animal in some prison. You shan't do for me as you have for so many others. There will be no drum rolls or black flags for the Constant Correspondent, you may put that from your mind altogether."

Chapter 11 – The Last Sacrifice

When Inspector Caldecott staggered into our sitting room a 8 o'clock in the morning the man looked as if he hadn't slept in a week, and in this case it was close to true. Holmes and I were not much better either.

"This case will be the death of me Gentleman," he said as he dropped upon the settee," then, realizing that his words were literally true where I was concerned, he stammered out a quick apology. "I beg pardon Dr. Watson."

"What news do you have for us?" Holmes asked without ceremony.

"He struck at St. Paul's this time Mr. Holmes. We've got no witnesses as yet, at least not who saw our killer anyway, but we've got several thousand who saw the gruesome results of his work before we could get it down."

"Another hanging Inspector?" Holmes asked.

"No Sir, it was the crucified Lord all over again, this time complete with a white linen wrapped about his middle."

"How is that even possible?" I demanded. "Did he not remove the man in pieces from the Romford Street flat? This man is the devil himself Holmes."

"He used the same system he used on Dick Lanier, across the street Dr. Watson. He had rope around the torso and then a series of half-hitches across the arms. The only difference was that this time he had a series of weights and pulleys already in place. He was able to hoist the sailor's chest up onto the second, pillared façade of St. Paul's in less than a minute by my reckoning, using a counterweight. Then a hook on the rope at each hand went into cables fitted with weights as well and in another minute the...body was raised to the top of the pillars. He made a neat job of it."

"A neat job?" I frowned, considering that we were talking about a human body.

"From the point of view of effectiveness, Doctor, nothing else I assure you, but he was there and gone in less than five minutes Mr. Holmes for a policeman who'd just made his round in front of the Cathedral was called back by the sound of the crashing counterweight that initially took the sailor's chest to the top."

"Why then would it have crashed down inspector? Since it had done its work in hoisting the chest up, it would have been on the ground."

"Right you are Mr. Holmes, but it appears our man used that method to descend the face of St. Paul's. Once he was on the ground he let go the rope and sprinted for his waiting carriage no doubt. The crash of the rocks upon the pavement alerted our constable on that beat and he, subsequently, traced the rope upward to where he saw the hanging man. That was 5:37 this morning. I was notified and found the situation little unchanged at 6:10, save for the crowd of several hundred onlookers who had gathered in the square below. The killer has learned and our work was made more difficult because of his use of cables instead of ropes for the weights which held the dead man up."

"Was there a placard this time?" Holmes asked.

"I knew you would want to see it," said he, pulling the thing from a burlap bag and handing it over.

"The sins of the father," Holmes read out, then handed it over to me.

"What do you make of that Mr. Holmes?"

"You were right Inspector; our killer has indeed perfected his method with practice. To place a man upon the front façade of St. Paul's in so little time is no small feat and having everything in place or ready ahead of time was vital."

"Exodus," I said.[25]

"Or Deuteronomy if I'm right," Holmes added.

"Sergeant Gallagher said it was from the Book of Numbers," Inspector Caldecott replied with a wry smile, "and he knows the Good Book."

"Have you determined the identity of the victim yet?" Holmes enquired.

"That will be a difficult task Mr. Holmes, for it seems that the killer, who has never been overly particular about injuring his victims prior to their deaths mind you, went out of his way this time. We are working on it though."

"The barbarity of this man," I began, but had no words to finish.

"And what of the press?" Holmes asked.

"Some of the boys were on hand by the time we finished but I don't believe any got a first-hand look at the scene. Of course, there was no shortage of witnesses who saw everything. We've been lucky in the past but I'm afraid this time your Correspondent may have bested us and you'll note how large the letters on the placard are this time. He meant for everyone to get the message."

"But as to that," said I, "what is the message?"

---

[25] Exodus 20:5, 34:7; Deut. 5:9-10; Num. 14:18; Jer. 32:17-18.

"You are familiar with the Bible verses Watson. Would you read one out for us."

I picked up my Bible and turned to a passage in Numbers and read.[26]

"The Lord is long-suffering, and of great mercy, forgiving iniquity and transgression, and by no means clearing the guilty, visiting the iniquity of the fathers upon the sons to the third and fourth generation."

"We've seen the Constant Correspondent kill some of the worst criminals in London," Holmes said.

"And most dangerous as well Mr. Holmes, don't forget that, for I tell you it's the talk of the Yard."

"Very true Inspector, but then he hung Fitzhugh Pomeroy in a church to shame the churchmen and kidnapped Justice Sir Thomas Phillimore."

"He wrote in one of his letters about you Holmes, and 'your allies in their uniforms, their fine robes, their scapulars, and ermines," I reminded.

"Yes," the Inspector agreed, "he said we merely traded on the suffering of the people, right?"

"So that covers the rank criminals, churchmen, and judges, so who is left for our killer whom he has not already addressed?"

"Well, I hate to say it Mr. Holmes, but Dr. Watson just quoted the letter and the only one I don't see represented yet is 'your allies in their uniforms.'"

"Correct Inspector. I believe you will find the

---

[26] Numbers 14:18.

dead man is someone quite familiar to you, a peer or superior from the Yard itself, perhaps. Someone with a long but chequered career. A man with a reputation for questionable results and, if we were to dig deeper, I doubt not that we'd find a man who lives far more comfortably than his official salary would allow."

Inspector Caldecott, for all of his bonhomie and camaraderie, had blanched noticeably and now sat in silence, staring at Holmes.[27]

"What is it Inspector," he said at last.

"You've just described Chief Inspector George Nathaniel Palmer, Mr. Holmes, all the way down to his golden signet ring you have! He trained me, me and half the men currently serving. He was our mentor."[28]

"Then this George Palmer is the 'father' the killer's message refers to," I explained, "and the killer is applying Palmer's 'sins' to the entire Yard, just as the verse applies it to the third and fourth generations."

"Only in our case Watson, the generations are not familial bloodlines, but rather each new wave of policeman coming into the Metropolitan Police."

"Gentlemen," Inspector Caldecott said, rising suddenly, "I must go."

"But we must press our case," Holmes said, standing and facing our trusted colleague.

---

[27] Bonhomie – a general cheeriness, kindly disposed, friendly.
[28] "The Rise of the London Police and the 1877 Scandal that nearly Shut Down Scotland Yard," by K. Odden, ©2021. Source: crimereads.com.

"I cannot Mr. Holmes. I must return to the Yard and see to this...scandal, for it will shake the very foundations, I assure you. It will shatter the public's trust in us. Parliament will...and the Queen. It may be the undoing of it all before it has run its course." Then he paused and looked up at Holmes. "I will assign Sergeant Gallagher and Constable DeJong to you if you feel you must proceed without me."

"I do," Holmes answered emphatically, "or else we'll find this bird flown and the cage empty."

"I will have them come here," he said, then his

voice grew low. "You knew it was him didn't you Mr. Holmes, Chief Inspector Palmer I mean? You knew he was the victim even before..."

"I don't know the Yard as you do Inspector, but yes, I thought Palmer the most likely target of all the men 'in uniform' known to me. His...missteps have been too well-known to be ignored."

The Inspector nodded soberly and it was only then I realized that this man, Chief Inspector Palmer, for all his faults, meant something to him. He had called him his "mentor" and that did indeed imply a kind of fatherly position. I wondered how it was that our correspondent had come to gain access to such information and how he had applied all the Biblical references so aptly to his victims. Then I remembered his words again and a cold chill came over me.

"The only thing that will comfort you in knowing this Mr. Holmes, is that all my victims are the very worst of men, selected for this one characteristic, and all are acquaintances of mine."

"Holmes," I said, after Inspector Caldecott had departed, "our correspondent wrote that all of his victims were 'acquaintances' of his. That would have included Chief Inspector George Nathaniel Palmer, but how is that possible?"

My friend was already deep in his own thoughts and I half expected his silence, but instead he raised his face and looked at me in the most penetrating way. Then he screamed that I had done it again, jumped to his feet, and raced for the door.

"You've done it again Watson!"

As he bounded down the stairs he yelled back that we should meet him in on Fieldgate Street at 10 o'clock and that I should bring my revolver.

I watched him from our window, racing down Baker Street all pell-mell and calling and waving for a cab. When one finally came near he jumped upon the step even before the driver had the chance to stop and called an address out to him. Then he was lost amid the hubbub.

I was left to wonder at my friend as I went to inspect my revolver. Sherlock Holmes was the most inscrutable man I'd ever known. That he was brilliant, especially so in the science of criminal detection, was undeniable, but also unfathomable, puzzling, and impenetrable, it went without saying. I had been with him now for several years, in the general role of biographer and de facto partner, and I doubted that I was any closer to understanding the man than I was on the day we'd met at St. Bartholomew's Hospital.

Still, there had been significant progress made in the area of our relationship, for in the early years it would have been impossible to have viewed myself as his friend, or he as mine, much less to introduce that notion in public. The years and the trials had, however, crafted a friendship between us which, if it was a union of contrasts, was sincere on both our parts. The phrase, "my good fellow," had crept into his vocabulary slowly and by degrees but it was clear now that it was a sign of appreciation and earnest affection.

I knew that I was not on Holmes level and yet,

despite this seemingly insurmountable obstacle, he had discovered something in me which was of great value to him.

He had first explained it by saying that while I might not be myself luminous, I was in fact a most excellent conductor of light.

"Some people," he stressed, "without possessing genius, have a remarkable power of stimulating it."

It was into this class that my friend deposited me, as it were, and he made it clear enough that he was much indebted to me for my contributions in this area. Now as the police carriage with a driver and my two official companions, the stalwart Sergeant Gallagher and observant Constable DeJong, made its way toward Whitechapel, I had time to consider Holmes' words, "You've done it again Watson!"

I had done it again and that "it" undoubtedly referred to my having once again conducted light and sparked his genius, but how had I done it? That was the perennial mystery that most often evaded me, but now I was intent upon figuring it out.

I tried to remember exactly what I'd said before he'd launched himself from his chair and raced headlong from 221B, much to Mrs. Hudson's chagrin. She frowned upon running on the premises and had waged a one-woman crusade to break young Billy, our page, of his habit.

I'd said that our correspondent had written in one of the letters that all of the victims had been acquaintances and that included Chief Inspector George Palmer. Then I'd asked how such a thing was even possible. From my point of view I could see no practical way for Monsieur Chartier's young clerk, whom we now knew to be our murderous correspondent, to have ever even met the Chief Inspector let alone known him well enough and long enough to honestly refer to him as his acquaintance.

It had been at this point that Holmes had screamed, jumped, and raced for the door. It was no use. When the carriage pulled up in front of the narrow, gated drive of St. Marys Church, I was no closer to knowing than I'd been when Holmes had said it.

Holmes was waiting there where we'd stood our vigil the night before and he came over and climbed in with none of the desperate speed I'd seen from him back in Baker Street.

"What is this then Mr. Holmes and what do you have that requires the two of us, for Inspector Caldecott said nowt about it."

"You are familiar with the bookstore just around the corner on the high street?" Holmes asked.

"Aye, Chartiers, a French chap owns the place, has for years now."

"That's the place," Holmes confirmed. "Well, Mr. Chartier has a clerk..."

"I know who you mean Mr. Holmes, Phillip Arderne is his name, a likable chap as I recall."

"Phillip Arderne," Holmes repeated. "He's our man and very deep he is in it gentlemen."

"He's the killer then Mr. Holmes?" the Sergeant asked.

"That he is and he's in Chartier's bookstore even

as we speak. Now I want the two of you to go in by
the front door," he said, motioning to the two
policemen. "Constable DeJong, you will assume a
post at the door to discourage our man from trying
that way. Dr. Watson and I will come in from the
rear entrance and meet you in the middle. I think it
would be best if you spoke first Sergeant. The usual
you know, suspected of something, taking him in for
questioning, then introduce us as consultants for the
police and ask the proprietor if we might have his
permission to search the young man's desk and any
other places he might keep things, something like
that."

"You know you put me in a tight spot Mr.
Holmes, I mean should my superiors ever find out
about this...activity."

"I understand Sergeant, but if I tell you that I will
take full responsibility..."

"Lots of good that'll do at the Yard, Sir, as they
can't fire you."

"That's right Mr. Holmes, the good Lord knows
that if they could've done that they would have, long
since," the young Constable added with a laugh.

"It's alright," the Sergeant said, "I'm good for it,
I just wanted you know what you were askin' of us,
it's a bit unusual."

"I comprehend that Sergeant Gallagher, but you
both know how important this is."

"That's why I said I'm good for it Mr. Holmes,
so we'll do our parts won't we Constable?"

"That's right Mr. Holmes, you can count on us."

With that we left through Plumber's Street and a

narrow passage at the rear of Chartier's, while Gallagher and DeJong went by Fieldgate to the high street and down the sidewalk straight to the bookstore.

Our way was the shorter but Holmes had to pick the lock and when we arrived upon the scene inside Sergeant Gallagher was just finishing his official sounding speech.

The portly Monsieur Chartier was deeply upset and shaken by the whole thing and I instructed him to sit back down at his desk and take slow, deep breaths.

"I don't understand Gentlemen," he said at last, "Mr. Arderne didn't arrive for work this morning. I've been worried as he has never done that before, a most dependable fellow I assure you."

"We need you to write down his address for us Mr. Chartier and if you have no objections, we would like to search the young man's desk and anyplace else he might use for storage," Holmes said calmly.

"He has a closet just there," he said, pointing to a portmanteau along the hall."

"Dr. Watson," Holmes said formally, "will you see to that and I'll search the desk."

"Dr. Watson?" the man said, surprised.

"Dr. John Watson," I replied, "at your service Monsieur Chartier."

"Then your companion here," he stammered nervously, "would be..."

"Mr. Sherlock Holmes," I answered.

"Mr. Sherlock Holmes," said he, reverentially.

"At your service," Holmes repeated. "Now you stay seated there and don't worry, we'll be done shortly."

As I turned to check the closet the Police carriage pulled up in front as it had been directed to do and I could see the proprietor swallow hard.

"Did Mr. Arden speak of any difficulties lately that may have interfered with his work?" Holmes asked.

"Never, Mr. Holmes, not a single syllable did he say upon that account. It isn't like him, that is, he has never missed work before, not in all the years he has worked for me. That is quite extraordinary is it not. I took him on when he was still a boy you know."

The closet held nothing of importance to our search, a suitcoat, an extra shirt, and a pair of well-worn shoes with a hole in the ball of the left sole.

"Anything Watson?" Holmes asked frankly as I reappeared.

"Nothing," I confirmed.

"Well look at these," said he, holding out a stack of papers without looking in my direction.

My eyes instantly fell upon the slanted script with the graceful sweep and regularity I knew so well from the letters of the Constant Correspondent and my muscles tensed involuntarily.

"Recognize those?" Holmes asked.

"It looks like a rough draft of one of his earlier letters," I replied.

"Indeed," Holmes agreed, "but what do we have here?" he said as he opened another drawer and

pulled a large, silver pistol out.

It was like no other weapon I'd ever seen, with a long, rifled-barrel and a nine-shot cylinder that revolved around what looked like a smooth-bore grape-shot barrel. I knew immediately that it was the weapon Holmes had described to Inspector Caldecott and me after the killing of Big Pat

Langford. It was the French-made LeMat Revolver.

"My pistol!" Monsieur Chartier exclaimed as he stood up, clearly agitated. "It's been missing for, for, I don't know," and with that he collapsed back into his chair and held his plump belly.

"Breath Monsieur," I implored in my doctorly fashion, "slowly and deeply."

"I'm afraid we'll need to take the pistol and the papers away with us Mr. Chartier," Holmes said, "I'm certain they have played a part in the string of recent murders across Whitechapel."

Monsieur Chartier nearly swooned at these words and his handsome head fairly flopped upon his arms on his desk. I turned and stared sternly at Holmes for there were times he could be brazenly insensitive to the condition of those around him.

He merely shook his head and went back to the desk and the last drawer.

"I say," said he loudly, "a 1-inch hemp rope and what is this? Have you ever seen this before Mr. Chartier?"

Holmes held up a razor sharp, triangular bladed knife with the finest of pinpoints which I recognized straight away. It was a foot and a half in length and deadly in appearance.

When the large man raised his head from his desk he nearly swooned at the sight of the weapon and groaned that he'd never seen anything like it in his life.

"It's called a beedak," I said in answer to Holmes.

"What's that?" said he.

"It's the Scots Gaelic word for a long-bladed dirk," I answered. "The fine point was designed to penetrate the medieval chain mail."

"Interesting," said he, as he prepared to place everything in a small case that had been sitting open nearby.

"Dr. Watson," Holmes called out, "can you come here?"

I looked over his shoulder into the open case and gasped.

"I say, white paint!"

After completing his search Holmes retrieved the paper with Phillip Arderne's address on it and put his hand kindly upon Monsieur Chartier's shoulder.

"I apologize most sincerely," said he, "for causing you such undue worry Mr. Chartier. We will leave you now, but should your man return please notify Inspector Caldecott at Scotland Yard immediately."

The poor man wiped his face with his kerchief and nodded obediently, but I couldn't miss the bloodshot eyes of a man who had been most sorely tried.

"You nearly killed that man yourself Holmes," I declared when we were all once again in the carriage and on our way to 17 Doveton Lane.

"I needed to see if he was hiding anything."

"That's some pretty damning evidence you've got there Mr. Holmes," Sergeant Gallagher noted.

"Yes, a fairly complete case in the desk alone. Throw in the valise with the white paint and the brush and you've got an sure conviction. All quite tidy and we haven't even searched his residence yet."

"Not a very shrewd bloke leavin' all that kit around says I," Constable DeJong opined.

"I would have to agree," Holmes said, handing the case full of evidence over to Sergeant Gallagher. "That should go a long way to seeing you clear of the woods Sergeant."

"Thank you Mr. Holmes, I'm sure."

Once we reached Doveton Lane the four of us tramped up a long flight of creaking, dusty stairs to the rooms of Phillip Arderne, our self-educated Constant Correspondent. The landlady turned the key and handed it to the Sergeant.

"See I gets it back before ye leaves an' make no messes, ee's a good lad!"

The paint on the four doors that opened on the landing, Arderne's and three neighbors, was peeling and the general air of the place was one of neglect.

When Holmes pushed the door open he just stood and peered in. The Sergeant did the same over his left shoulder and the Constable likewise upon his right.

"I'll say," Sergeant Gallagher offered, "not what I was expectin'."

Finally they entered and I, who had brought up the rear, got my first glimpse into the inner sanctum of a killer.

Now I understood the Sergeant's comment. The main room wasn't large but it was bright and clean, with fresh paint all around. It had one large window at the end and this was draped with a heavy fabric all the way to the floor. It was the kind that would block out the cold quite nicely. In front of this was a small oak desk of the slanted top variety which could be opened to a compact storage space beneath. The whole thing was meant to aid in writing and was, ironically, called a "clerk's desk." A comfortable chair was tucked neatly under the desk, which Holmes was now bent over and examining papers.

A small coal burner stove sat along the wall and a wicker settee with several cushions stood opposite across a small, worn Persian rug. A picture of the Queen, cut from some periodical, hung in a cheap frame above the settee. A large bookcase along the wall to the right of the main entrance and formed the fourth wall of the sitting room. Through an archway across from the main entrance was a long narrow room split into a small, curtained bedroom on the right, where Sergeant Gallagher was rifling through a compact bureau, and a smaller kitchen on the left where Constable DeJong was inspecting the silverware. A little square table and two chairs sat in space between the kitchen and bedroom.

"A neat chap, this Arderne fellow," Constable DeJong noted. "I wish my wife kept our place half so clean."

"She prob'ly could if you weren't such a chore," the Sergeant said with a laugh. "Take a look at this Mr. Holmes," he said, emerging with a square of white linen folded up neatly. "This is the same stuff the hanging man had 'round his middle."

"Really?" exclaimed Holmes. "Your certain?"

"Dead certain," said he.

"Interesting," Holmes replied. "And I've got more roughs of his letters here Watson. A prolific writer, most assuredly, who makes two or even three drafts for every one he sends us."

"That does seem strange," I said, looking at one of the sheets. "These are as neat and flawless as our own. He certainly doesn't need the practice."

"Yes, but...wouldn't a fellow like this get rid of the evidence once the letter was sent? And the fabric too? Why hold on to it all?" Constable DeJong asked.

"He probably never dreamed we'd put the noose 'round him like we have. Thought he was safe as the Bank of England he did!"

Chapter 12 – Holmes' Gambit

A letter in the now dreaded sweeping script was lying upon the mat upon our return.

"It was hand-delivered," I declared. "There is no post mark or stamp."

Holmes looked behind him, up and down the street, but it was impossible to know who might have delivered it or even how long it had lain there.

We found the morning papers upon the table in our sitting room and I grabbed one and sat down wearily in my chair. We had now been going a full week without adequate sleep and yet Holmes, as was his way when upon a case, seemed energized.

"Read the letter first would you Watson?"

"Well, well, well, Mr. Holmes. You walked right past me when you left the flat on Fieldgate Street and Romford. By the miserable look upon your face I took it you'd been fooled by my change in tactics. I always enjoy the comments of the crowds around my little endeavors. They are such an odd mix of superstition and stupidity that one can only hope such folk never gain any important positions in our government, otherwise we will all be lost. You never thought of St. Paul's did you, but even you must admit that I provided you with adequate clews. Our work together is nearly complete now Sir and all that is left is the promised finish. What will become of us then Mr. Holmes? For you I imagine only dark days ahead, for it must be admitted that a Sherlock Holmes without his Dr. Watson was an altogether negligible fellow and a forgettable man. Remember how few knew your name before le bon docteur joined you, and how few cared. You will recede back into yourself and your worst parts will predominate once again. The inevitability of it all, of you Sir, is all so droll. Dr. Watson will be mourned by all who knew and loved him, mainly for his patience and longsuffering with you. You will bury him with a stately marble gravestone, one with the little vines around the edges and the words 'noble friend' and 'never forgotten,' but it will be me who, after a short wait, possesses your friend's skull.

As for me I will go on in the rosy glow of my success, knowing that I have met and indeed bested the greatest detective of all time and left him a shell of his former self. I wonder if it would not be a mercy to provide you with the same end I granted Chief Inspector George Nathaniel Palmer, but then that would be to leave the people with a memory of you at your apex and we cannot have that, can we? Enjoy your morning paper Mr. Holmes. You will be seeing me again very soon. CC"

I could tell this letter had upset Holmes' usually unperturbable mind when it came to his cases and he lit his pipe and sat back in silence.

I folded the letter and returned it to the envelope wishing I could toss it in the grate, for the man's words were like a knife every time I read them. No one could overlook his comments regarding my skull either, a thing to which I was understandably still quite attached.

Holmes' gambit was to take the fight to the killer and push him into the corner where, if he had meant what he'd said, he would end the matter of his own accord.

Even as I reached for the morning paper his words coursed through my mind.

"If you succeed in running me to earth, I shan't be taken in nor will I swing for what I've done...I am quite resigned to my fate, should it come to that."

"We've rattled the cage Watson," Holmes said suddenly, as if he'd read my mind.

"I would say we've done far more than rattle the cage," I declared, "for while we didn't take the man himself our search produced the needed evidence."

"Perhaps," he nodded.

"Now it simply requires the police to close the ports to him and launch their search. No doubt the indomitable Inspector Caldecott has already done that."

When I opened the paper my breath caught in my throat as I read the banner headline and I froze.

After a minute Holmes spoke somewhat impatiently, waking me from my paralysis.

"What does it say?"

"CHIEF INSPECTOR MURDERED."

"Well," said he after another long pause, "read it out."

"Chief Inspector George Palmer, long a leading figure at Scotland Yard and just coming up on his thirtieth year with the Force, was discovered hanging from the highest pillars on the front façade of St. Paul's Cathedral in the hour before sunrise by a number of passers-by. The killer, as yet unknown to the Police, had positioned the victim in a familiar and, for some, a sacred position, one reminiscent of that of the crucified Savior upon the hill of Calvary. Upon his chest was a sign which read, "SINS OF THE FATHER."

"This reporter isn't sparing his audience much is he, but one wonders how he knew the identity of the dead man prior to the running of the morning presses, when Inspector Caldecott sat right there upon our settee at 8 o'clock this morning ignorant of the same."

"Indeed, he was sincerely stunned when you

identified the man as his own Chief Inspector. So how was it done?"

"You read the last letter Watson, 'enjoy your morning paper Mr. Holmes.'"

"Do you mean that the killer somehow got Palmer's identity to the reporter?"

"More than that my good fellow, for a reporter knows better than to print unverified statements, let alone those which come from anonymous sources. You will notice Watson, that when he tells me to enjoy my morning paper he doesn't designate which one he is speaking of?"

"And as we take three most mornings how could he be certain we would read the one he had informed?"

"For the simple fact that he communicated his information to multiple reporters from enough of London's papers to make his statement, 'enjoy your morning paper,' a mathematical likelihood."

"But as you said Holmes, a reporter knows better than to print unverified statements, let alone those which come from anonymous sources, so how did he convince them?"

"He had the body did he not?"

"Yes, but even Inspector Caldecott, who had known the man for years, was unable to identify it."

"If he had the body Watson, would it not hold that he possessed the golden signet ring which Inspector Caldecott spoke of? Along with it would come the man's pocket watch, which doubtlessly had his name somewhere upon it, his initialed watch fob, and all the man's identifications."

Once again I was left to marvel at Holmes' keen reasoning and astuteness of mind.

"With such things enclosed in sealed envelopes and delivered to their doors by hired men at predetermined times in the early hours, even somewhat earlier than the body was actually raised into position, an anonymous source might be very persuasive might he not."

"And we know the body was completely stripped," I acknowledged.

"And the face was..."

"All to make identification impossible for the Police."

"Just so Watson. To make it impossible for any personnel from the Yard to identify the man. The golden signet ring and a written letter from the killer no doubt was enough to convince one of these reporters to make the early paper."

"Perhaps the watch went to another and the watch fob to a third," I exclaimed.

"And the wedding ring to another."

"This is all most diabolical!"

"But you must appreciate his ingenuity Watson, for the Constant Correspondent was not going to be put off this time. He was certain of that and he took all the steps necessary to insure that the papers would be his tools this morning."

I opened the Illustrated Police News and there was another story, this time far more salacious.

"CROOKED SCOTLAND YARD OFFICIAL SLAIN," I read out.

I unfolded The Morning Post and read its clear

headline, "KILLED AT ST. PAUL'S."

"Inspector Caldecott was correct wasn't he," Holmes muttered between puffs of his pipe. "This scandal will shake the foundations of the Metropolitan Police before it has run its course."

"And you know it won't take much to destroy the public trust," I commented. "It looks like the Constant Correspondent will get his way after all."

"Well, maybe some good will come of it yet."

I read all the papers we had and each said more or less the same thing, railing against corruption in the police force and demanding immediate action and accountability. It seemed that Chief Inspector Palmer's dubious reputation as a chancer willing to get in on the take was too well known for Scotland Yard to even mount a defense. As a result, at least during the first day, their official statement was no statement at all.

Holmes went out for a couple hours around lunch, saying he needed activity, and returned more silent than ever. Shortly after, Billy came in and gave him a telegram, which he read, crushed in his hand with what I can only describe as a satisfied growl, then slipped into his inside jacket pocket.

Inspector Caldecott joined us in the afternoon and events had rendered him a much-changed man.

"What now Mr. Holmes? For to tell you the truth I can no longer see myself clear in this perverse, grotesque case. I've notified the ports and set the search for young Mr. Phillip Arderne of 17 Doveton Lane, Whitechapel, but I'm all through believing we can take this devil. He's killed six of

London's most dangerous or most experienced men and he's made it look easy. It's like he's mocking us, giving some kind of class on his sick, twisted methods, nailing men to crosses with railroad spikes, hanging them from churches, even Tower Bridge. It's a nightmare," said he, and it didn't take much to see that the murder of Chief Inspector Palmer had fairly undone our friend.

"Calm yourself Inspector," Holmes said in that authoritative way he could take even with a Prime Minister. "For what would you say if I told you that we were now in the final hours of this nightmare and that the sunrise always follows the night."

"Can you mean it Holmes?" I cried, thrilled beyond my wildest imaginings, for to admit it I had begun to share in the Inspector's hopelessness.

"Where the life of Dr. John H. Watson, M.D., is involved, I never jest," Holmes said with a smile.

"Then what Mr. Holmes? What must I do for I am all eagerness to put this dog down."

"Our killer will be at Chartier's tonight at 8 o'clock Inspector," Holmes announced with a confidence that stunned us both.

"The Constant Correspondent?" I said.

"Indeed Watson," said he. "You will place men outside the back door Inspector, in case he makes his escape in that direction, but remind them that this is the man who killed Big Pat Langford with that unique revolver and they must take him down without hesitation."

"I will Mr. Holmes and while they might have let the man go happily for the killing of Langford, they are steeled to deal with him now. Whatever you may think of Chief Inspector Palmer," he snarled, "to a man we agree he deserved better than he got."

Holmes nodded and proceeded.

"A ladder from the roofs along there comes down near Plumber's Street and it is just possible that our man could escape that way."

"I'll post four men with Sergeant Gallagher at the back door and two men there, at the ladder," the Inspector said, writing notes in his little book.

"With at least two men outside the front of the store, I'd like you, Inspector, to enter with us."

"I'll bring my revolver," I replied.

"That would be wise," Holmes said quietly. "Your men will guard the front in case he makes it past us. Now the store's three main aisles run back into the building. I'll take the right-hand as we go in, as that aisle cuts off the hallway to the back door. Watson, you'll have the left-hand, which leads to the stairway, the upper floors, and the roof. He must not get past you."

"He won't," I promised.

"Inspector," Holmes smiled, "the easiest way out of that place is the front door..."

"And the easiest way to the front door is the center aisle. You can rest assured Mr. Holmes, that this killer won't be going through me."

"We took the LeMat revolver away with us when we searched the premises, but I labor under no delusion that this man will have another pistol of some sort on hand, for he has promised us he will not be taken."

"I'll warn all my men. We'll be ready to do our part if it comes to that, Sir. You can count on us."

"Good, then the only thing remaining is to set the time for our arrival. The store closes at 8 sharp and I expect no customers, still we must be prepared for innocent bystanders when we rush the door. We must arrive at 7:55 sharp at all stations, rear, side, and front, then the three of us go in at the rush.

"What will we do if there are still customers?" I asked.

"We'll put everyone to the ground, for their safety and ours, then we subdue the killer."

"It sounds like a good plan Mr. Holmes. I suppose if the Police carriage calls for you at 7:20 that will give us time."

"Yes but you must not be later."

Darkness had fallen by the time we climbed into the carriage and rolled away toward Whitechapel and Chartier's bookstore. I was glad to finally be doing something toward bringing this whole thing to an end. The Inspector had called it a perverse and grotesque case and I shared his sentiments. It was the sort of thing that would be best to have behind me. We all did a final inventory of our weapons and, satisfied, settled in to get our minds straight for what lay ahead.

Halfway there Holmes looked across at me and said, in little more than a whisper, "All things are ready, if our minds be so."[29]

---

[29] Henry V, act IV, scene 3, by William Shakespeare.

It was a line spoken by the King in one of Shakespeare's plays and I nodded. After the horses had gone on a little farther I gave the reply, the Earl of Westmoreland's retort.

"Perish the man whose mind is backward now!"

With these few words we made the entire trip, arriving five minutes ahead and drawing off upon Alder Street where we were invisible to the store.

Holmes confirmed that everything was in order and looking across Whitechapel High Street to the other side he pointed out a waif sitting upon the walk and playing with his worn cap. I rightly guessed it was one of Holmes' irregulars.

"That signal tells us there are no customers left in Chartier's," Holmes said, "are you all ready?"

There was a murmur and general nodding and with that every man dispersed to their stations.

When we rushed through the front door there was no sign of Phillip Arderne anywhere, still we rushed on and looking up from his desk Monsieur Chartier leaped to his feet with a speed no one of his condition could muster, spun upon the Persian rug and made for the hallways to the back door. This confused me to no end but I pressed on trying to keep up with the Inspector, while Holmes had outpaced us both.

Then to our utter amazement, Holmes slid to a stop facing Chartier himself. He'd cut the man off from his escape, I held the stair and Inspector Caldecott blocked the center aisle. I was still confused and my eyes searched for Arderne without luck. Holmes held his little silver revolver on the big

man the whole time while they glared at each other.

"What is this Mr. Holmes?" the Inspector asked brusquely, for he too had expected Phillip Arderne.

"Behold the Constant Correspondent, Inspector Caldecott. This is our man as sure as I am Sherlock Holmes."

I felt that my friend had finally gone wrong, for in his wildest dreams Monsieur Chartier could not have outrun Sherlock Holmes upon the streets, alleys, and byways of Whitechapel the night we rescued Justice Sir Thomas Phillimore. It simply couldn't be. Then the man spoke.

"You have bested me Sir," said he, "but I wasn't going to live here as a slave to the gangs and I told you I would never be herded about your prisons like a base animal. I would like to have known how you figured it, for I believed it a perfectly crafted thing, but alas..."

Then, with the most incredible speed, Charles Chartier grabbed Holmes by the wrist of his gun hand and held it perfectly still. He didn't try to turn it aside but seemed to be struggling against Holmes to keep pointed just where my friend had it, directly at Chartier's own heart.

The handsome Frenchman smiled at Holmes as my friend tried unsuccessfully to pull away from him.

"Goodbye Mr. Sherlock Holmes," he said with great solemnity, as if they were the oldest and best of friends or else, that he knew those words would be the last he would ever speak. Then he raised his free hand and placed his index finger against Holmes' trigger finger.

The two men stood like this for a moment in silence. They had faced off in one of the greatest challenges I'd ever witnessed. They were two giants, both brilliant in their own way, but there could be only one winner. Then Chartier pushed upon the trigger.

Even though I'd witnessed the whole event, the loud explosion of the pistol took me by surprise. When I looked again the man whose presence had commanded the stage for years and had made London jump in fear, lay in a heap at Holmes' feet, dead.

"I've got this from here Mr. Holmes," Inspector

Caldecott said, stepping in immediately and taking the revolver from my friend's hand just before his men rushed in.

Now in charge of the scene, the Inspector told his men that the killer had taken his own life just as they closed in. To this news a great cheer went up and a general congratulating was carried on among the men.

I still understood as little as I believed Inspector Caldecott did and try as I might I could not clear it up in my mind.

As he escorted us from what was now fully his crime scene, the Inspector was clearly elated.

"If I called upon you at 3 o'clock tomorrow, I suppose you could explain this whole mystery. As things now stand I'm as confused as a man could be, but never fear Mr. Holmes, for my report will be the simplest I've ever written and I feel a certain light-heartedness about that."

"And your superiors will congratulate you."

"No doubt," said he. "No doubt."

Chapter 13 - The Man No One Knew

Holmes had been out most of the day, no doubt celebrating his success in his own unique way, listening to an orchestra with his eyes closed and returning just before the appointed hour to explain everything. It was not a moment too soon either, for

I had made no progress at all in resolving the many contradictions that existed in the incredible case of the Constant Correspondent. It had been all I could do simply to wait for the explanation that would sort it out.

Holmes began by speaking of the surprisingly clement weather we had been having, "despite the odd cold evening." To my amazement he continued on to discuss the upcoming horse racing season. It was a topic upon which I had never once heard my friend speak and yet, as he proceeded I found he possessed a surprising depth of knowledge. He discussed the 2000 Guineas Stakes in Newmarket, the Epsom Derby in Surrey, and the St. Leger Stakes held in Doncaster, the three races that made up the English Triple Crown. He even went so far as to predict that Ormonde, and not Saraband, Minting, or the highly favored, The Bard, who was everyone's favorite, was the horse to watch.

Only when I heard the bell go did I realize he had simply been filling the time, occupying us with other topics while he waited.

When little Billy showed Mr. Phillip Arderne in, however, I was shocked.

The young man seemed thinner and, in light of the news of his employer's suicide, paler than ever.

We shook hands all around and Holmes offered him a seat next to Inspector Caldecott and a freshly brewed cup of tea.

"You directed that I should wait upon you at this hour Mr. Holmes," said he hesitantly, "but I am afraid I'm ignorant of the purpose."

"In light of...what has recently transpired with Mr. Charles Chartier, and your central role, I thought you should hear the details of the case."

"If I was central to Monsieur Chartier's plans, which I in no way can credit, I was ignorant of it, I assure you most vehemently."

"Ignorant?" the Inspector replied skeptically. "Did you not hire the murder carriage and supply the driver with instructions?"

"I did, I hired the carriage," the young man admitted with such open earnestness that I realized beyond doubt that he could never have filled the role of our mad killer. It was simply beyond him and his landlady's words came back to me.

"See I gets the key back before ye leaves an' make no messes, ee's a good lad!"

Without knowing it at the time she had given us the truest description of the man before us we were ever likely to receive. He was clearly "a good lad," and little more, save for those fields which Chartier had spoken of as being the young man's areas of academic specialty; history, the natural sciences, Egyptology, and the Orient."

"I followed Monsieur Chartier's directions to the letter, as was always his expectation that I would. He required the carriage and sent me to acquire it. It was no different than when he told me a few days ago that I would be going to York to purchase several lots of books for our store. He had always done the purchasing before, but I obeyed without question and went off upon the train."

"You knew Mr. Arderne was innocent even

when you told Sergeant Gallagher and Constable
DeJong about the clerk didn't you? You knew he
wasn't the killer," I said, confronting Holmes.

"This case presented several challenging points,"
Holmes admitted. "For one, I direct you to the idea
which we were asked to believe from the outset, that
this young man was the acquaintance of all of the
victims. By the time we rescued Justice Phillimore,
however, the proposed sixth victim, I had to ask
what incredible must have been required to make
Mr. Arderne the acquaintance of so highly placed a
personage. Whereas Chartier himself might have
had a case before Justice Phillimore, we had already
been led to assume that his complaint against the
Justice was solely due to the latter's failure to punish
Fitzhugh Pomeroy, the poisoner. My investigation
upon this point revealed that Chartier had in fact
lodged a case of complaint against the McAuley
Gang's 'collector,' Abraham Bram Stibbe, long
before the Pomeroy Poisoning Case."

"That's correct Mr. Holmes," Arderne replied,
"and the Justice ruled against Monsieur Chartier."

"Yes, seven years ago," Holmes agreed, "at a
point in his life when Mr. Chartier still believed in
the law and was still trying to solve his Whitechapel
problems through the medium of the courts."

"Well, it seems he learned the futility of that," I
remarked.

"You are invaluable Watson," Holmes declared,
"for that is exactly what occurred. Mr. Chartier
learned that the law would never touch the men who
extorted his hard-earned living as well as that of his

neighbors. These were also the men who, when it came to it, didn't hesitate to beat or kill those who resisted them. The fact that Mr. Chartier survived after his case against the McAuley's wasn't due to luck was it Mr. Arderne."

"No Sir, he had to pay them double the original amount and for a time it looked grim."

"He feared he was finished, did he not?"

"Yes Sir, he did."

"The turning point was complete when he grasped the fact that a good citizen, deserving the full protection of his government, was simply left to the gross exploitations of the criminal classes. According to his wife, an exceptional woman whom I met with earlier today, several experiences like that of Justice Phillimore had jaded her husband on the idea that a bright future lay ahead for them. I believe it was at that point that he began to put his past experiences to work in preparing for his ultimate revenge."

"What do you mean Holmes, what past do you speak of?" I asked.

"I sent a telegram to Paris some days back," said he, explaining the return telegram I had seen him receive that very morning. "It confirmed my suspicions that our man had played some rather substantial role in the French Theatre. There he was known as Danton-Charles, as the stage was not considered a fitting vocation for an aristocrat. Through this alias the elevated name of Chartier was not besmirched."

"And what did they find Holmes?"

"Danton-Charles dashing good looks had made him quite the star of the stage in his younger years and upon the merit of that success he purchased a second-rate theatre which he had soon transformed into the La Grande Métropole."

"The Métropole was a leading theatre for quite some time" I began, then recalled its sad fate, "before it burned."

"And without the happy precaution of insurance at that Watson," Holmes added, "it left Mr. Chartier at the mercy of creditors, with no means of making good."

"Let me guess," Inspector Caldecott interjected, "Mr. Charles Chartier soon arrived in London."

"Where, with the sale of his wife's jewelry, he was just able to purchase a failing bookstore, which he subsequently transformed it into the esteemed Chartier & Company."

"Just as he had created the Métropole," I said.

"Not quite on the same grand scale nor with the same degree of public adulation for which the Métropole was famous," Holmes replied, "but yes, Watson, similarly. The importance of all this was obvious to me from the first. It meant that I was dealing not only with a skilled and successful actor capable of carrying off his role, but also with a theatre owner and manager who had successfully written and staged a multitude of his own plays. Plays which, I might add, were famous for the twisting plots and surprises which delighted his audiences and made the Metropole one of Paris' favored entertainment spots."

"It may sound strange to say this now, after hearing all of this from you Mr. Holmes, but I can see the influence of the theatre in his crimes."

"And among the things the Métropole was most famous for Inspector, was its dramatic sets and the theatrical staging of the actors. This upheld the presence of the French language on display in his letters. Working with Mr. Chartier would have exposed Mr. Arderne to the language to a degree far beyond the norm, however, that would not explain the natural usage of phrases like 'le bon docteur' and 'how do you say, the rude awakening!' As I told you earlier, our words declare our connection with a group. An Englishman would have said, 'How do 'we' say?' The use of the term 'á contre-sens' was just a mistake. Mr. Chartier simply let his guard down for a moment and once it was done, being a native speaker of French, he lacked the mechanism to recognize the error. A Frenchman wouldn't have seen the issue with it and an Englishman couldn't have missed it."

Inspector Caldecott had said our killer was holding a class on how to kill, but as I saw it now, it was Sherlock Holmes who was holding the class on the science of deduction. We all sat in rapt attention as he discussed the case.

"Two of our earliest pieces of evidence actually pointed in opposite directions, that our man was lightly built and approximately 5-foot 7-inches and yet had no trouble lifting a two-hundred-pound anvil which would have challenged even a far larger man."

"The contradiction might be overlooked in one instance, even though the man who could do it would be far stronger than the average man of that height and light build. There are exceptions among men after all. When this aspect of our killer was repeated however, then it became increasingly hard to overlook. The strength required to lift the anvil was one thing, but to lift a human body off the floor is another. To lift the herculean form of Abraham Stibbe from the floor and bear it 150 feet out upon the catwalk of the Tower Bridge, that was something else completely. It called for a deeper examination of the case."

"One thing puzzles me still," I confessed, "and that is how a large man like Monsieur Chartier, who could be described as portly even, could stay ahead of you upon the chase Holmes. In his shop he was so easily out of breath, even to the point of fairly fainting and having bloodshot eyes?"

"As to that Watson, one of the easiest things for a thin man to manipulate is a bulky appearance. It may be changed very easily with the addition of padding and the correct articles of clothing, but a man's height is not nearly so easily managed. Believe me, I know of what I speak."

"And that's just what our post-mortem found Mr. Holmes," the inspector offered. "The man had the body of a practiced athlete, trim and strong, but he wore a large, hand-sewn, padded belly with straps over the shoulder and around the back."

"I learned as much when I retrieved the paper with Mr. Arderne's address on it. At the time I put my hand upon Mr. Chartier's shoulder and it confirmed the presence of a deep indentation in the muscle exactly where a strap holding up a substantial weight must go. Now this depression was not the result of weeks or even months of wearing such a thing, but of years. So the question becomes, when did Mr. Chartier begin putting on weight Mr. Arderne?"

The young bookseller sat silent and puzzled. Everything he was hearing from Sherlock Holmes was new and unheard of, literally. That his boss had been a mad killer was more than he could fathom.

"Years Mr. Holmes."

"Before the court case or after?""

It was...afterward," he mumbled almost as if to himself. "Just after, Sir."

"I forward that his plans first began to take shape then, when he began to modify his appearance."

"To what end Mr. Holmes, for what would the gang care about his weight?"

"That's just it Inspector. His weight alone was a chief factor in leading Dr. Watson to disqualify the man as our killer. Along with this, pretending to be out of breath and winded is a simple task and one of the first lessons an actor learns. One may achieve the effect of bloodshot eyes by simply holding the breath and resisting the attempt to blow it out. A minute of that and it's a rare man who will not have the red eyes associated with all manner ailments."

"I also examined his right shoe when I put my hand upon his shoulder. The patent leather pump was quite in the bright light and revealed a barely visible but plain reddish line along the full length of the shoe. You may recall the water main break which flooded the street next to St. Paul's upon the night before the murder of Chief Inspector Palmer. There was still some standing water along the walk on the day of the murder and the soil there, being of a unique red-orange tinge, is quite obvious. In the rush to complete all that was necessary that night, our man overlooked his shoes. It is easily done and has happened before has it not Watson."

"Indeed it has Holmes," I seconded.

"So you knew that Chartier had been there, at St. Paul's that is, and within the timeframe of our murder," the Inspector stated.

"It was elementary, I assure you."

"But were you not swayed by all of the evidence against me Mr. Holmes, for Madame Chartier told me of your findings," the young man asked.

"It seemed the final nail in your coffin did it not Mr. Arderne? Yet it was a grave mistake."

"How so Holmes?"

"How could so exacting and diligent planner as our Constant Correspondent had proven himself to be, be so unaware of the incriminating evidence he left all around, apparently just waiting to be found? And if he had not done it, then who had? Who had access to Mr. Arderne's desk and, eventually, to his home? Who had the power to send the young man away at the critical time? Everything pointed back to Mr. Chartier. It was this point which confirmed all my doubts, but I must admit that the most critical break in the case was tied to your right index finger

Mr. Arderne."

"Yes," I said, "after my visit to the bookstore I told you about the black ink upon his right index finger."

"But why would such a small thing bear such significance to the case Mr. Holmes," the Inspector asked.

"I've found that it is often the smallest details which bear the most profoundly upon a case," Holmes answered. "In this case Watson, can you imagine a right-handed writer with such a stained finger, writing a letter, folding it, putting it in the envelope, sealing the envelope, and then posting it, and all without getting a single black mark or fingerprint upon either the letter itself or the envelope, even over the course of several letters."

The effect of these words left the three of us in Holmes' audience speechless and it was a silence that was only broken after an entire minute when Inspector Caldecott, in essence, spoke for all of us.

"This is witchcraft Mr. Holmes! Witchcraft pure and simple Sir, for do we not all see what you see and yet, seem to see nothing? I know you and Dr. Watson went over everything with a fine-toothed comb, as did I, and never did we find a single telling mark upon any of it."

"That was the moment that proved this young man's innocence without question," Holmes said, "everything else was just so much confirmation. Even the writer's use of the double-C's, as you noted Inspector, was too much. It was another attempt, just like the staged evidence in and around Mr.

Arderne's desk and at his rooms, like Mr. Chartier's feigned exclamation, 'my gun,' the comment that his clerk was largely self-taught, the fainting spell, the labored breathing, and the bloodshot eyes, all to prove that the writer was in fact trying to 'set up' the innocent Charles Chartier as the murderer."

"But Mr. Holmes, I do not consider myself to be self-educated," Mr. Arderne said, "for it was Monsieur Chartier who took me from the street and showed an interest in helping me. Even while I worked for him in the bookstore every day was filled with more lessons. How could such a man then plan for me to be the scapegoat of such repulsive and heinous crimes. I simply cannot accept the picture you have portrayed for us."

"Yet I assure you that it was not only his unquestioning intention to lay those crimes upon you Mr. Arderne," Holmes said, "but also to kill you, his own protégée, at the end of the process. Upon your return from York this morning he would have notified Inspector Caldecott as any good citizen would and just as he had been instructed to do, but before the police could arrive you would have committed suicide. Mr. Chartier could then construct whatever fable he desired to explain your action. After all, he'd prepared us all along for just such a suicide, writing as you he said, 'I shan't be taken in nor will I swing for what I've done.' Perhaps he would say that when you saw all your things taken, including the revolver, you were distraught. 'It was then he realized the game was up Inspector, and in a moment I heard the loud bang of a pistol.'

After a short investigation and inquiry, Chartier would been utterly free to go on as he wished."

"But how did you know I had gone to York, and hadn't carried out the St. Paul Murder?"

"Ah, that," Holmes muttered, "that was a bit recherché.[30] I noted a slight fragrance upon one of the pillows upon your bed, Mr. Arderne, which I deduced could only have come from a woman. You see, even if a young man had been sworn to secrecy by his employer, as I assumed you had..."

"Yes," Arderne admitted, "Monsieur Chartier said there had been a series of robberies where people had announced they were going to be away and he warned me not to make the same mistake."

"I simply reasoned that even if you had refrained from broadcasting your trip, it would be impossible for you not to tell your sweetheart. The lady proved very protective of your secret I might add and only when I had described your situation did she relent and confess all to me Mr. Arderne."

"But how did you know the woman where to find the woman Holmes?" I inquired.

"A quiet, reserved young man, who spends the bulk of his time at work and the little remainder in his residence. A man who did not frequent the public houses or other establishments, whose main diversion was reading, and who had a limited circle of friends. The odds were...astronomical as to who the woman would be Watson."

Mr. Arderne heard these words in silence, with

---

[30] Recherché – unusual, odd, obscure.

a reverentially bowed head.

"I must second the Inspector's praises," he said at last, "for what I have just witnessed has been the most magnificent demonstration of the power of logic and deduction which I have ever witnessed Sir. I confess myself doubly in your debt."

Holmes sidestepped the young man's tribute with the same ease he used his famous two-step in boxing and continued discussing the case.

"If there were any doubts left regarding Mr. Arderne, they were easily resolved. Where, for instance, did you spend your day when Dr. Watson came in and purchased his volume on the Yarkand Expedition?"

The dark eyed man thought for a moment.

"I was in the shop all day Mr. Holmes. That wasn't unusual for me and, as I recall, Monsieur Chartier had to step out for a few hours."

"What time would that have been, when your employer had to step out?"

"He left at 9 o'clock and was back around 2."

"And would you be surprised if I told you that he had spent a good deal of that time on Fieldgate Street between Romford and New Street?"

I knew immediately what Holmes was saying. Chartier had changed his tactic that day and rather than waiting for night to commit his murder, as we had assumed, he made use of the room near Romford Street to murder Chief Inspector Palmer of the Yard.

"You see, your employer went so far as to identify himself in his letters Mr. Arderne. As if to confirm your view that you were not wholly self-taught, he proudly declared, 'I am a good teacher,' and yet, as Dr. Watson pointed out, for all the boasting, the man suffered from the same malady as most of his countrymen, he had no concept of the English paragraph."

"I confess myself hurt Mr. Holmes, to find that Monsieur Chartier truly meant to use me to cover his crimes. How could the man who, for all practical purposes, raised me, have turned so completely against me?"

"Are you not aware of any failing upon your part Mr. Arderne, which might have been the cause of a change in your mentor's attitude toward you?"

A long silence followed as both men stared at each other as if neither the Inspector nor I existed.

"He was unaware of any such failing in me, of that I am quite sure."

"I would propose that he was neither as ignorant as you have assumed Mr. Arderne, nor as forgiving as you might have hoped he would be."

"What are you gentlemen talking about?" the Inspector demanded. "For you've lost me along the course."

Holmes looked at the Phillip Arderne as if to say that the decision to disclose his secret was his and his alone and the young man shifted uneasily on the settee.

"I'm afraid, Inspector, that the woman you know as Mrs. Chartier is the owner of the fragrance Mr. Holmes spoke of earlier."

Chapter 14 – The Strange Case

A very few words will suffice to conclude a case which Sherlock Holmes considered one of the five strangest cases ever to come before him.

Although I resisted the Case of the Constant Correspondent for years I cannot deny that it provided my friend with a vast canvas upon which to demonstrate his unique gifts and skills.

His opponent was just as Holmes had so rightly judged him; a man torn between his own two parts. In this Charles Chartier truly was not that different from Stevenson's Dr. Jekyll and Mr. Hyde. Like Dr. Jekyll, Chartier had a keen intellect, wonderful skills, and a good heart. Like Mr. Hyde he was a monster from the darkest pit imaginable, bent upon murder and revenge in their most grotesque forms, leaving trail of destruction in his wake.

There was a final twist to the case. Chartier had declared there would be 7 victims, "all the worst kind of men," and if Holmes was unable to stop him, then I would become the 8th victim. Holmes, however, had seen through the shroud of darkness which the brilliant Frenchman had hung over so many of his works. He comprehended that the 8 victims Chartier had disclosed were but a partial list and, in a diabolical twist, were there to obscure his 2 main victims.

Chartier had learned of his wife's love for his lowly clerk, Phillip Arderne, and it didn't take him long to discover that her sentiments were returned. In creating his plan, the entirety of his crimes were meant to be laid incontrovertibly upon that young man. Phillip Arderne was always intended to be the undisclosed 9th victim. In the cruel depths of his "monster self," Chartier had envisioned the ultimate torture for his wife, the 10th victim of his wrath. Her punishment was to be the living of a life without the man she loved. Chartier knew that every day lived like that would a horrible kind of living death for his wife and he would be there to witness it. This is the darkness Holmes had seen into and revealed for the rest of us. Little did Charles Chartier realize that his wife had already been sentenced to that punishment once before, as the darkness in him had destroyed the man she'd loved.

In a letter from Mrs. Chartier which was received some weeks later and which included a picture of her late husband sitting trim and handsome with the LeMat Revolver upon his lap, she wrote in part:

"You have freed him from the agonies of his life Mr. Holmes...he was a man tormented by so much. He never shared his feelings, but a wife always knows when there is trouble in the soul of the man who shares her bed. My poor husband's tortured soul was filled with a darkness and a poison so great that it slowly overcame the most wonderful man in the world. In the end I no longer recognized my poor Charles. Without my knowing it, he had died somewhere along our difficult path. All I knew was that the creature he left me with was a monster. Even if it still possessed his face and form it was void of the man I had loved. I send the picture for rememberance sake."

The death of Charles Chartier was put down as a suicide and passed unnoticed into the history of Whitechapel. His killing spree, for such it was, was never connected publicly as the work of one man loosed in London. Inspector Caldecott's reports are all that remain of the official story.

In the end both Holmes and Inspector Caldecott were proven right. Holmes believed that some good might come from the grotesque crimes of Charles Chartier and it did. Inspector Caldecott thought the scandal that would follow would destroy the Metropolitan Police and it did.

The scandal which erupted from the murder of Chief Inspector Palmer created so great a public outcry for reform that Parliament was unable to ignore or weather the storm. Even the Queen, it was rumored, had made her own demands.

By mid-year a dozen Inspectors had lost their positions and half of that number were prosecuted. Year's end brought a new system of enforcement in London, as the findings of a commission created specifically for reform were enacted.

Inspector Caldecott received a commendation for his "effective handling" of the "spate of wild crimes" which gripped the city during that spring.

Phillip Arderne and Eugenie Chartier married in a June wedding from which Holmes and I received some white cake. Chartier's & Company Books became Arderne's Booksellers in September, the original sign being sold to be used for roof repairs on a neighboring hotel. So it was that the Chartier name vanished from Whitechapel for good.

I still visit the place from time to time and I never leave without at least one new book under my arm. There are new clerks today and I rarely have the opportunity to talk with the proprietor, whom I'm told has several new interests in the city as well as several young children.

When May arrived I forced Holmes onto the train and we made a day of it at the races at the 2000 Guineas Stakes in Newmarket. He was obvious as one of the few gentlemen not wearing a top hat. He did, however, win a tidy sum on a racehorse named "Ormonde," who, just as he had predicted, went on to great things, winning the English Triple Crown.

The End

Thank you for reading:

"The Constant Correspondent"

COMING SOON

What's next for Holmes & Watson?

Malcolm Findley was a strange little man with a large, pale, half-bald dome of a bulbous head, a trailing mane of silver-white hair, and a pair of Belgian-made golden pince-nez eyeglasses. He was also brilliant and this aspect of his personality so overshadowed the former that he was considered a colossus.

Born the eldest son of a poor fisherman on the Isle of Lewis in the windswept northwest of Scotland, he grew up in a stone cottage with a thatched roof that didn't blow away in the frequent gales only because it was held down by a net of hemp ropes weighted at the ends by stones. As a boy he taught himself to read and write by using the only book his parents owned, a Bible, which he then memorized. When he left home he told his mother not to worry over him saying, "I'll be a professor at university" and in five years he was.

When Sherlock Holmes first met Professor Findley the older man scolded the great detective for not using distilled water in his chemical experiments, calling it "slipshod work." Then he quoted one of Holmes' earliest monographs, en toto, on bicycle treads and used it as proof for the existence of a higher power. Now an old man, the Oxford Don of whom Holmes once said, "he understands," has vanished.

The only clue is a half-finished sentence on a chalk board. What has happened to the esteemed professor and can Sherlock Holmes find him? Once again, the game is afoot but this time Holmes and Watson don't even know where to start.

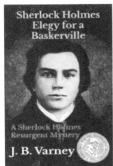  

The Sherlock Holmes
Resurgent Mysteries

Elegy for a Baskerville
The Dreadnought Murders
The Deadly Cleric
The Tenth Man
The Constant Correspondent
The Oxford Don
Coming Soon

available at amazon.com

The Cat & The Professor
Mystery Series
by J. B. Varney

The Professor Who Wrote Upside-Down
The Professor Who Knew a Postman
The Professor Who Drove an Aston Martin
The Professor Who Climbed a Mountain
Murder on the Green Mountain Express
Murder by Fiction
Death Rode a Red Vespa
Death in the Heather
Book 8 – coming soon

available at amazon.com

ABOUT THE AUTHOR

J. B. Varney "discovered" Sherlock Holmes as a boy. It was a time when none of his peers had read even one of Sir Arthur Conan Doyle's mysteries. Thus began his life-long love of mystery and twisting plots.

Mr. Varney is a historian, genealogist, and descendant of many of the ancient families of Europe whose names grace the pages of his Sherlock Holmes mysteries.

"The game is . . . still afoot!"

Made in United States
Troutdale, OR
04/22/2025